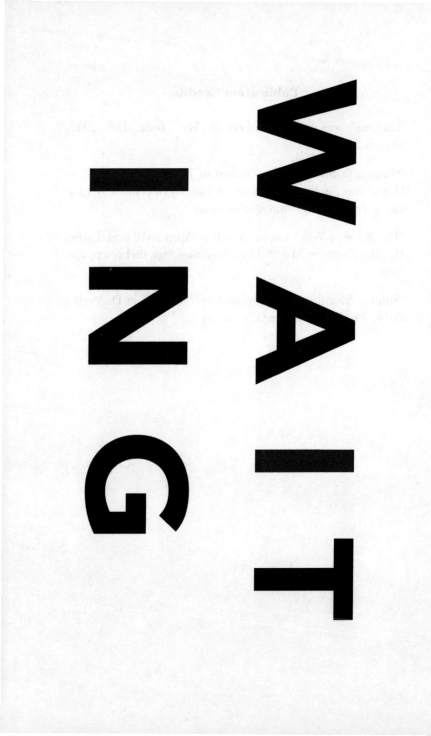

Publication Credits

'Lingerie' was first published in *Muse India*, Dec 2015. museindia.com

'Sharmaji's Shoes' was published in June 2016 and 'Aab-e-Hayat' was published as 'Water of Life' in December 2013 in *Out of Print*. outofprintmagazine.co.in

'The Rapist's Wife' was published in April 2018 and 'Ladies Waiting Room' in May 2018 in *The Brown Page*. thebrownpage. com

'Sunday Morning' was published as 'Garbage' in December 2011, *The Daily Star*. thedailystar.net

To my city that will always be Allahabad

NIGHAT
GANDHI

WAITING

*a collection
of stories*

ZUBAAN
128 B Shahpur Jat
1st Floor
New Delhi 110 049
Website: www.zubaanbooks.com
Email: contact@zubaanbooks.com

10 9 8 7 6 5 4 3 2 1

ISBN 978 93 85932 54 0

Zubaan is an independent feminist publishing house based in New Delhi
with a strong academic and general list. It was set up as an imprint of
India's first feminist publishing house, Kali for Women, and carries
forward Kali's tradition of publishing world quality books to high editorial
and production standards. *Zubaan* means tongue, voice, language, speech
in Hindustani. Zubaan publishes in the areas of the humanities, social
sciences, as well as in fiction, general non-fiction, and books for children
and young adults under its Young Zubaan imprint.

Typeset by in Baskerville 11/13 by Jojy Philip, New Delhi 110 015
Printed and bound at Gopsons Papers Ltd

Contents

1

Lingerie

I am seeing a therapist, because I have no interest in having sex. I feel ashamed and anxious whenever my husband approaches me. All I want is to be left alone. He's a good man who never forces me to do anything. After a few months of dwindling intimacy between us, he mildly suggests that I seek professional help.

—⁂—

Bruce is my psychotherapist. I'm seated on a big, motherly couch in his cozy office, facing him and his lamps and plants. His manner is genteel, his voice soothing. I am in the United States where it's okay to talk with a stranger about sexual problems. Bruce uses words in a gentle, almost priestly manner. He makes appropriate eye contact, leans forward slightly, his body language geared to suggest empathy, and listens as if he really cares to listen, not just because he's getting paid for it. He asks me what brings me to him. I start crying. He hands me a box of tissues.

'I'm not sure why I'm not attracted to my husband any more,' I say, wiping my tears. 'What's my problem?'

Bruce shifts the conversation from my present to my past. 'Tell me a little about what it was like growing up in your family.'

I try to piece together the patchwork of my family history – what it was like to grow up back home as a girl in a hyper-religious household set within a conservative, middle-class Muslim family.

'It was about being extra good, extra polite, extra obedient. I thought marriage would free me. But all my friends thought the same and they all ended up like me. Suffocated.'

'Suffocated?' Bruce leans in.

'Yes. Suffocated.'

I'm trying to be concise, but my mind wanders among vignettes of life with my authoritarian father and subservient mother. My mother's reason for existing was to fear, resent and please my father. As I'm talking, I suddenly have a heightened sense of the injustices my mother had faced. I am more educated, more resourceful than her. I married the man of my choice. Yet I seem destined to walk in my mother's footsteps.

At the end of my first counselling session, Bruce explains my problem. His interpretation seems a bit far-fetched, but I listen.

'You were a victim of emotional incest,' he begins. 'You were your father's favourite daughter. He was married to you emotionally and used you to fill the vacuum in his marriage with your mother, but you couldn't fill that vacuum forever. When you went ahead and got married, you betrayed your father. You are still trying to come to terms with what you did. You're still trying to win back your father's approval.'

That dark, dense cloud of despair swirling in my gut – could it be explained so simply?

Back in our apartment, I repeat what Bruce has said, while I prepare formula for my daughter and heat up leftovers for dinner.

My husband feels victorious and validated by Bruce's words. 'Haven't I been saying the same things to you?' he says. 'Your father still rules your head and heart. And you won't become an adult unless you make a conscious effort to get him out.'

I feel bewildered. Am I not an adult? I need to become an adult by shifting loyalty from father to husband? I, a victim of emotional incest, must tear my father out of my head and heart and replace him with my husband. Was that all I needed to make me an adult?

—∽—

'So you think my father is at the bottom of my problems?' I bring up my doubts with Bruce in the next session.

'That's my hypothesis. The first-born daughter has a special and complex relationship with her father and it's even more complex if there's an emotional vacuum in the parents' marriage which she has to fill. It's natural to feel guilt over betraying your father.'

'It's not guilt. I feel like I've betrayed myself.'

'In what way have you betrayed yourself?'

'I feel like… I haven't figured out who I am or what I want from life. I'm tormented by thoughts of where my life is going and especially after my daughter's birth, I wonder if it's going anywhere at all. Jumbled thoughts race through my mind all day. How can I change that? How can I gain some control over my mind?'

Bruce's suggestion: 'Symbolically divorce your father. And reclaim your husband as your lover. Work on your real marriage – the one with your husband.'

'Divorce my father?'

'Yes. And bring back the missing romance in your marriage.'

'How? Is that going to help me answer my questions? Some days, I feel my patience has run out. I don't know how long I can go on like this. I just want to leave everything and run away. I fear I might do something utterly stupid.'

Bruce doesn't delve into what sort of stupid things I might do. Instead, he asks me about my daily routine.

'Okay,' he says, when I finish. 'But what do you do on Friday evenings?'

'The same. Cook dinner. Bathe my daughter. Put her to bed. Read a little or watch TV. Go to bed.'

'That's what needs to change. What you and your husband need is a change. Get a babysitter, go out to the movies, invite your husband for a candlelight dinner on the weekend. You have to pursue your husband as if he's the only man you want. Make yourself look attractive. Get yourself new clothes, buy some lingerie. Dress sexy for him at bedtime.'

Dress sexy? My stomach heaves and the muscles in my abdomen knot. I love my husband, but do not wish to sleep with him. Change my daily routine? Most days, my routine is my wisp of sanity. I fret about not having enough hours to do everything on my checklist. Feeding, nursing, bathing, cooking, laundering and clearing up keep me going. My routine is my killer, my saviour.

I am driving home from my second appointment with Bruce. It is a misty, weepy-grey December evening. The weak winter sun has vanished early from the small Texas town we have recently moved to. Christmassy coloured lights are strung across the bare branches of trees, brightening up the staid exteriors of houses. Holiday cheer can't lighten the greyness of my heart. My husband has taken the afternoon off to babysit. If he babysits more, does more laundry and cleans the bathroom, I just may summon up the energy to feel more excited on Friday nights. How can I explain the connection between housework and sex? Sex is not meant to be compensation for housework. My husband has counter-explanations. He too has to work hard at his job. He is our provider.

Bruce's suggestions rumble in my gut as I wait for the traffic lights to turn green. Shame, guilt, nausea, anxiety and self-loathing churn inside me. Images of skimpily dressed mannequins rise like skinny ghosts in all their silkiness, laciness, smoothness and flatness. I, a fretful mother, with my pear-shaped, post-partum body, have no place to hide from those ghosts. I say I'm not obsessed with thinness or flatness, but I obsess over thinness and flatness of tummies all the time. My milk-engorged breasts versus the inviting, smooth and firm breasts of the skinny ghosts! If you can hold a pencil under your breasts, they are sagging, I had read in a women's magazine. I can hold half a dozen pencils undermine. I wish to be a woman who is in control of her life. I feel in control of nothing.

Bruce is trying to help me, but I am feeling weepy and insulted. I see unattainable perfection receding from me like a vanishing dream upon waking. I feel stripped down to my drooping breasts and nursing bra stuffed with nursing pads. I am bulging hips and ungainly fat under my nondescript sweaters and pants. The stubborn, resistant little girl inside me grows livid. *Dress sexy? That's like prostituting yourself!* Bruce has hit where even the power of my inner girl can't save me. I won't be able to do what he has suggested. I don't tell my husband about Bruce's bring-back-the-lost-romance idea. I fear he may rush out to Victoria's Secret and come back with something scarlet, satiny and frilly for me.

One night, after my second appointment with Bruce, I dream of my first boyfriend. In the dream, I meet him at some nameless mountain resort. He is as good-looking as he was in high school. His demeanour sleek and murderous, his face dark and sharp – enough to make me jelly-kneed. But when he starts to speak, something goes wrong. He tells me he has had six kids with his wife.

'How could you do this to the poor woman?' I ask angrily.

He smiles his boyish, made-to-win-women's-hearts smile. And in the next moment, he tries to kiss me.

I push him away. 'You never really cared for me, did you? Or anyone else. You only cared about getting kisses.'

He doesn't deny it. I feel hurt by his lack of denial. I wake up and thank God it was a dream and I'm not the one with whom he had six kids.

In the next session, I tell Bruce about my interpretation of the dream. 'Maybe, my ex was trying to hint that I should have an affair or something?'

'I don't advise my clients to have extramarital affairs. They create more problems than they solve. What you give to a lover has to come out of what you are meant to give your husband. So the scales tip in favour of the lover and this inevitably spoils the marital relationship.'

Bruce is a sensible, respectable, salt-of-the-earth kind of man. He's like a priest reciting prayers by the side of the dying. He is a warm, old quilt it's safe to huddle under. I imagine he's a very considerate and conscientious husband who does the laundry and takes out the trash without being asked.

A few days after my boyfriend dream, I wake up early on a Saturday morning, while it's still dark, hours before my daughter will awaken. My husband is away appearing for job interviews. My body aches for more sleep, but I haul myself out of bed. My radio alarm clock is tuned to news. News of war and rape and refugees from Somalia, Bosnia, Palestine, Lebanon makes up my wake-up call. There's war in all parts of the globe, except in my safe and small existence in this small Texan town. Guilt and gratitude make me spring out of bed.

I start the coffee maker and enter the living room. I pick up a literary magazine I have borrowed from the public library and start reading the interview with Tennessee Williams, in which he claims he would stay up all night to write with the aid of black coffee. I imagine staying up all night with a thermos of black coffee. I can barely stay up half an hour after putting my daughter to bed. I put down the magazine, fetch a cup of coffee and turn out the lamp. I sip coffee in the dark and rest my head against the back of the couch. The walls and the dark wooden bookcase filled with unread books are my attendants. Dawn pours in through the living-room window. I gaze longingly at the softness of this dawn, beyond the sharp, brown branches of bare oaks. Soon, too soon, the cries of my daughter end this purposeless reverie. I embark on another day of chores. Why must I read and envy another writer's writing routine? A thousand thoughts have marched across my heart like marauding soldiers, pronouncing me dead. Tennessee Williams is writing my obituary: 'Her life was made up of details. Disgusting, unavoidable details. She could never muster courage to say no to details, so how could she stay up nights writing, in the service of her craft?'

—⁓—

'How are you finding your sessions with Bruce?' my husband asks, when he returns.

I've been going to Bruce for a couple of weeks now.

'I don't know.'

'Aren't they helping at all?'

'I don't know. You would be the first to know if they were!'

'I think you should see him a few more times, before you give up.'

So I continue seeing Bruce, but after my sixth session, I decide I've had enough. I'm driving to what I have decided will be my last session. I haven't passed the litmus test yet: I still have no interest in having sex.

'How are things going?' Bruce asks, smiling, looking fatherly.

'Kind of bleak, to be honest. I haven't made much progress.'

'Even though you've been trying out some of the things I suggested?'

'Well, we went out for dinner once or twice, but...it didn't lead to anything else.'

I shrug and stare at the potted plants on the windowsill. I don't mention the lingerie I didn't buy. Nor my failure to pursue, tease, tickle and titillate the genie of romance into the bedroom.

'Well, some people just don't have much of a sex drive,' Bruce pronounces, as we are ending our last session. 'Maybe, you're one of them. Maybe, you'll never find your husband very attractive and you'll just have to accept it.'

I agree with his conclusions. I feel like I'm attending my own funeral.

I nod like a schoolgirl eager to please her class teacher. He's right: maybe, I'm just dead sexually.

'I guess you're right,' I say. But the girl in me protests. *Wait! There's more to this story. I'm not the only one responsible.*

'I don't want to sound pessimistic,' Bruce continues, 'but as long as you have a good marriage in other ways...'

As long as I have a good marriage in other ways – that's a good way to end! What else could you say to a happily married woman who loves her husband, but is not interested in sleeping with him?

—⁂—

I'm spooning baby food – pureed pumpkin and green peas – into ice trays. I make and freeze my own baby food. I had tried pureed sweet potatoes and green peas with my daughter. She spat it out. I tried mixing the veggies in her cereal. She still didn't care for sweet potatoes or peas. She lunged at the spoon and spattered the yellow-green gruel all over her dress, on the carpet and the rest on her high chair. But I don't give up. I try out different combinations of vegetables, fruit and cereals. I read to her, I sing for her, I make flash cards to get her to say words; and when she gratifies me with her babble, I reward her with hugs and kisses.

My old friend, my spirit guide, calls. We used to see each other often, before my husband and I moved to Texas. She always has soul food to offer. But this time, even she doesn't offer much.

'I have no desire for sex,' I tell her.

'Well, it's only natural,' she says. 'It's your hormones. You've just had a baby. And you've also just moved. You've taken on a lot. You're exhausted. Be kinder to yourself.'

'It doesn't feel like I'll be okay. Ever,' I say, swallowing the lump lodged in my throat. 'It's not about hormones or the baby or the move.'

'What do you think it's about?'

'It's this constant restlessness. It pervades everything in me. I don't know what to make of it. My therapist said I had to bring back the lost romance in my marriage.'

'How?'

'He asked me to divorce my father, to whom I'm apparently emotionally married, and pursue my husband. Try going out for dinner dates with him and dress sexy at bedtime.'

I hear what sounds like a muffled laugh. 'Well. Did you? I can't imagine you... How's your relationship otherwise?'

'Not terrible. We have our good days and our bad days. He could help more around the house. I feel tired all the time and I just want to be left alone. He's worried about finding a job next year. The other day, we had an argument. I sat in the parking lot outside a McDonald's for an hour. I only came back because my breasts started to leak.'.'

There is no shortage of desolate days. We are unpacking boxes the movers have left in the living room, when he suddenly gets up and says he has to go to work. It is a Sunday afternoon. What work do you have on a Sunday, I ask. Work, is his reply. I retreat into the silent fortress of my rage.

When he returns a couple of hours later, I ask for the car keys. I have nowhere to go. I drive around the dark streets of the strange town where the only two people I know are my husband and my daughter. I am afraid of getting lost, of straying out too far. I pull into the parking lot of a McDonald's and sit listening to the radio. Rectangles of yellow light spill onto the pavement from the eatery's white-frosted windows. Inside are children and adults enacting the very familial mime I wish to run away from.

An unknown mountain cottage in some far-off forest beckons. It is a small, sweet-smelling forest and my room is filled with books, paintings, rugs, a coffee maker and a stove. I am going for a walk. Returning. Eating breakfast. Reading. Writing. And each day is morphing into the next, until I have had my fill. I will then return to husband and child.

But I am sitting in a car outside a McDonald's and two insufferable men are guffawing about automobiles on a radio car show. Sitting out there hasn't helped me with my smouldering questions. It is madness to desire contrary things. If I didn't want to cook, clean or take care of my daughter, if I wanted to be left on my own, why, then, did I want a husband, child and home?

It is time to go back and nurse, say my leaky breasts, my timekeepers.

When I push open the glass door of our living room and enter, I see them before they see me, the only two people in the world who matter to me. He is holding a stuffed toy in his hand and she is sitting on his lap. They are my refuge from a scary, uncaring world. All I want at that moment is to become the missing piece of this puzzle.

On New Year's Eve, I am the one to suggest we build a fire and get a bottle of champagne. I want to start the new year with a new attitude. We lie on the rug in front of the fireplace, sipping cheap champagne and watching the Duraflame log burn out its promised three hours in the grate. I have fed and bathed my daughter and managed to sing and put her to bed early.

After the log has burned out and we have finished the champagne, he tries to kiss me. I turn away.

'Can't I even kiss you any more?' I can hear the sadness in his voice.

'I'm just not ready for it,' I say.

Despite the fire, despite the champagne, the heart isn't ready.

—⁓—

Winter's over and I'm watching the oak's pale green buds from the living-room window. I now have a Mexican cleaning lady who comes twice a month. I'm taking my daughter to a babysitter three mornings a week. That's all we can afford. During those mornings, I try to read; I try to write. But most often, I just while away my time writing in my journal aimlessly. There are forty boxes still waiting to be unpacked. The unopened boxes on the living-room floor compete with baskets of unfolded laundry. This week is harder on my nerves. My daughter is home because of an ear infection and the cleaning lady is down in Mexico re-wedding her husband of ten years in a proper church ceremony. There's laundry, there's dishes, there's vacuuming, there's dead leaves... I sweep up the dead leaves. My daughter is learning to crawl and the floor has to be kept clean. She's not eating much, rejecting the vegetable and cereal combos I create for her. I get mad when she does that, but I also can't get over the miracle of her.

'My back hurts and I feel like I've lost my mind!' I break down when my husband calls from work to check on his wife and daughter. Bitterness spills out. 'I know the dirty house and the laundry don't mean a damn thing to you. You can just walk out and go to work. But I can't.'

'You're not being fair,' he responds calmly. 'You don't have to be so angry. I'm trying my best to help you. You should realize I also have a lot to deal with. If I don't find a job here, we have to pack our bags and go back to India in six months' time. I can't lean on you if you crack so soon.'

Can't lean on me? How could he be so dead certain, say this with such calm?

'Should I give up my research and apply for some other kind of job, so we can stay on in the US?' he asks gently.

'No, you mustn't give up the work you love,' I say. 'I don't want to be the one messing up one more thing in your life.'

'I want you to be happy.'

He ends up making me feel guiltier than I did before and lonelier than ever.

I know what his work means to him. 'I won't be happy if you sacrifice your work for my sake,' I tell him.

'Do you think you could be happy in India? Should I say yes to the Indian offer?'

'What choices do we have?'

There aren't too many.

I will remember his face just before he said 'yes' to that offer. It is the face of an innocent boy who is making difficult choices in a cruel, pragmatic world. I hug him, because in that moment, having said 'yes' for his sake has given me an opportunity to redeem myself, to transcend my selfishness in denying him other kinds of happiness.

My big questions remain, as does my restlessness. They bloom with time. Time can neither wither nor kill them. They are a part of the brokenness of existence. I am just one shard among millions. I will go on tending the questions in between housework mingled with ideas, yearnings and the heart's hunger – what can I do except tend this heart like a shrine?

My husband says I can write anywhere, at any time of life. All I need is a desk, pen and paper. My meddlesome yearnings can be put aside for now. I have to train myself to be patient and resigned, wait till my daughter grows up and everything is more settled. I pray to God to remove all traces of selfishness in me. May I become someone he can lean on. May God prevent me from complaining about boxes and dead leaves and unfolded laundry. And the dread of repeated moves.

The girl in me continues to protest. *I'm not a plant to be uprooted and transplanted into new soil every so often and be expected to thrive and grow. I need time and space and steadiness to thrive.*

But her protests have to be silenced. Life can't be allowed to become totally chaotic.

2

Shaming. Shaving

She recites the paaki prayers, steadies the razor and gets ready to sweep it across the triangle of soaped pubic hair. She's already done with the armpits. She always does the armpits before tackling the pubic hair. It's less disgusting. Abba's discarded blades, collected by Ammi, aren't the best tools for taking care of pubic hair; so she resists shaving that area.

She always ends up with scrapes and cuts. Every month. She presses the razor down hard, using the fingers of her free hand to stretch and tauten the skin. Ouch! A fresh cut. Blood oozes from it. She pours water over the cut. She re-soaps the unshaved part and runs the razor over it again.

'I hate it. I hate it!' she mutters, wincing between tears.

Some long, tough hairs have got wedged inside the razor's flap. She flips the razor open and holds it under the running tap. But the force of the water won't dislodge the hairs. She has to use her fingers to pull them out. Her stomach heaves at the very thought. She avoids looking at the crinkly hairs swirling towards the shower drain. The air in the bathroom is humid and still. The hairs whirl and vanish through the little round opening. She washes the razor with soap and dumps the rusty blade. It won't be of any use at all next month. She stares at the triangle of pubic skin. It looks like a mown lawn. Only a few hairs remain along the lips. She hasn't touched them for fear of cutting herself. She stores the razor in the cabinet under the bathroom sink and steps back into the shower stall. Water runs down her body and washes away the sweat and dread of the last half-hour. She emerges after a long shower, shaved, cut, clean.

'Why do I have to do this every month?' she musters the courage to ask Ammi.

'How else will you become paak? You can't pray unless you are paak and have removed the napaak hair. Every girl has to do it.'

'I will never do it once I leave,' she swears under her breath.

Every month, Ammi interrogates her about the paaki bath and asks if she had recited the paaki prayers before shaving.

'Have you bathed? Have you shaved?'

She nods without meeting her mother's eyes. She disappears into her books to avoid such conversations. Rage is held in place by stony silence. She dips her head into her books and presses her legs together to make the itching and burning go away.

She wants to ask the few friends she has at school if they also take a paaki bath and shave, but shame gets in the way. If she asks, she'll have to tell them about her own periods and paaki bath.

'You mustn't talk about these things. It's shameful,' Ammi has repeatedly warned.

Why? Why can't I talk about it with other girls if all girls get it? It's a question she wants to ask Ammi, but she can guess what her mother will say. So she doesn't bother.

At night, pressing her legs together to deaden the itching, she converses with her imaginary mother, the one she can turn to with just about any question, the one who listens with an open mind to even the silliest of them. After saying her isha prayers, she lies in bed in the dark and asks silently: *Why*

*do I have to shave? Am I going to have to do this all my life? I'm not
doing this ever when I leave this house!*

Praying comforts her and in order to pray, she has to follow
Ammi's purification rituals. She fears her prayers won't be
accepted by God if she prays unshaven.

Her grandmother has taught her to pray. 'If you pray,
you'll find peace,' Dadima says.

Dadima is like her imaginary mother, but not in every way.
She can't talk to Dadima about everything, like her periods or
why she has to shave.

'Unless you pray and ask for help from Allah, things will
never change,' Dadima has told her.

She's afraid that if she doesn't pray the right way, nothing
will change and she will have to go on shaving the rest of
her life. She never misses a prayer. Maybe, if God were very
kind, she'd stop having periods or her pubic hair would stop
growing. Even if it is midnight and she is up late, studying for
a test, she never goes to bed without saying her prayers. When
her forehead is resting on the red velvety prayer mat that was
Dadima's gift, she feels safe like she did when she was a child
and would rest her head in Dadima's lap, burrowing into the
folds of her soft cotton saris that smelled of her kitchen.

—m—

She removes the roll of her dried blood-soaked pads, wrapped
in newspaper. She hides the roll under her dupatta and trots
off with her bundle of shame through the silent, napping
house. She has let the bundle grow fatter with every pad she
stuffed into it, so she would have to throw it out only once.
Dried stale blood, musty newsprint, moist fresh blood and
sweat – the smells of shame – cling to her. The long, steamy
afternoons in the bathroom, with sweat trickling down her
face, sweat sticking to her thighs – she's been squatting to
wash the rags and hanging them up inside the cabinet to dry.

The rags take several days to dry inside the closed cabinet, but they can never be hung out in the open. They are tainted with unremovable stains. And it would be shameful to hang them out. She uses them to wrap the cotton pads which she cuts out from a thick roll of cotton given every month by Ammi. She has mastered the art of tucking in the ends of the rag into a waistband and securing both ends with safety pins. She hates collecting unwashed rags and washing them. Ammi cuts the rags out from old bed sheets and petticoats. She hates reusing the used rags. But Ammi won't hear of throwing them away after just one use.

She peeps into the kitchen to make sure the cook isn't there, before darting out the back door. He has a way of questioning her which makes her want to hide. As if he knows things she doesn't want him to know. She squirms at the mere thought of him asking her: 'What's that bundle you're carrying in your hand, Bibi?' She doesn't like the way he speaks, the way he leans so close to her that she can smell his paan and cigarette mouth when he bares his brown teeth at her.

Her mind is crammed with 'what ifs'. What if the cook sees her? What if she doesn't reach the garden wall in time? What if she could have another mother? What if she could stop having periods? What if she didn't have to take the paaki bath every month? Ammi has told her only girls get periods. She hates the secrecy around the whole thing more than the fact that boys don't have to go through it. She has noticed bra straps showing through the school tunics of the other girls. But how can she possibly ask them about periods, shaving, bras? Nobody talks of such things.

She reaches the back-garden wall and rises up on her toes, her hand stretched out over the wall, and tosses the newspaper bundle out into the empty lot on the other side.

She hears the bundle land with a thud and nimbly runs back into the house through the kitchen door. Nobody has seen her. She is safe. It is all over till next month. How shameful it all is! Shame hoods her like a thick, dark, suffocating curtain.

Then for several months running, she doesn't get her periods at all. She is relieved she is not napaak and won't have to shave. She tells Ammi about this. But one day in school, she suddenly feels the creepy wetness between her legs again. She worries about it all day. What should she do? Can she tell one of her friends? What if the blood stains her white shalwar? Then everybody will come to know. So she doesn't move much and can't understand a thing of what they are taught that day. She can only pray that she gets home safe, unnoticed. But when she is walking with her classmates to the sports field, she suddenly feels someone touch her on the shoulder.

'You've got a stain.'

'Oh!' Shame wells up within her.

'Do you need a pad?' the girl asks casually.

'Umm, yes. Where can I get one?'

She is caught. Oh God, now everyone knows she has her periods. Now she won't be able to hide it.

'Come with me to the school office,' the girl says.

Hot shame seeps down her spine as she walks a few steps behind the girl, so as not to have her see more of her stains or answer her questions. They reach the school office and the old nun there hands her a pad. Nobody – the nun, the girls in her class – seems to think much of her stained shalwar. They behave as though it's an ordinary occurrence. But then, they probably have mothers who went to school. Ammi has never been to school.

The pad the nun has given her is slim and narrow, so she can hardly even feel she has it on. It doesn't feel like a heavy, padded door sitting between her legs, the way her own pads do. Over the thick cotton pad she usually wears, she pulls on panties to keep the pad in place. She suspects everybody on the planet knows she is wearing a pad, that she has her period, from the wobbly, waddly, unsure way in which she walks. It isn't as if her mother can't buy the slim sanitary napkins from the market. But buying them from a shop would mean asking a man for them; and that would be shameful.

She comes home that day when school is over and announces to Ammi that she wants pads like the one she got from school. She says she will no longer use those thick cotton pads wrapped in pieces of cloth cut out from old sheets and petticoats. She wants the slim pads she can even carry in her schoolbag and then she won't have to face those horribly embarrassing accidents, even if her periods start without warning.

Ammi argues. She says she has used the homemade pads all her life and what is wrong with them? They are much cheaper.

But she stays adamant. 'I won't use cotton and those rags any more,' she declares, the suppressed anger over her shameful memories welling up again.

—∞—

'Do boys get it?' she asks Ammi.
  'No.'
  'Why not?'
  'I don't know. Only girls do.'
  'Why do only girls get it?'
  'That's the way Allah made girls.'
  'Why does Allah do bad things to girls?'
  'What do you mean?'
  'Like giving girls periods. Does it ever stop?'
  'When you're old, it'll stop.'
  'How old?'
  'I don't know. Quite old.'

She thinks of Dadima. *When I'm as old as her*, she wonders. Dadima is really old. *Maybe, I'll have to wait another fifty years*, she calculates gloomily.

Ammi doesn't like Dadima, because she holds her responsible for all the fights that she has with Abba. Ammi has stopped her from going to Dadima's on weekends, after she started her periods. She thinks she has a good excuse which doesn't make any sense. Ammi says she has become a big girl. It seems that going on weekend visits to her grandmother's, where she had played with her boy cousins, could, somehow, lead to losing her izzat, now that she's a big girl.

'A girl's izzat can be destroyed in a second if she makes the slightest mistake,' Ammi had warned her.

The definitions and boundaries of izzat were never explained to her. Nor was it made clear how or why a girl could lose her izzat in a second.

'How does a girl lose her izzat?' she wanted to know.

Ammi hadn't answered the question. Instead, she had said, 'A man can dance naked in the streets. Nobody cares. But a girl has to guard her izzat or she can lose it in an instant. If I don't teach you these things, who will? People will say this girl's mother didn't teach her a thing.'

She has had to accept that a girl's izzat is fragile as china and a man's indestructible like steel. She has never seen men dancing naked in the streets. But she's got Ammi's point: if a man were to dance naked in the streets, it would be fine; but if a girl danced naked in the streets, she would lose her izzat instantaneously.

After the monthly bleeding, followed by the shaving ritual, is over, the burning and itching still take a few days to subside. She has learnt to sit in class, her legs tightly pressed together, bending down when the itching becomes unbearable, pretending to pick up a pencil so that she can give in to the urge to scratch herself down there without being seen. Under the fresh, raw cuts, the growing stubble is beginning to poke through. The hair just never stops sprouting.

—∾—

Ammi questions her, looking to her for answers now, just the way she herself used to look to Ammi for them when she was a child. She can't satisfy her, though. She's become her mother's mother. She's a matter-of-fact, terse, abrupt and often, impatient nurse.

Her mother is seventy-six now and of increasingly wobbly gait and wandering mind. She holds up her shalwar for her daughter to inspect.

'It has bloodstains, so can I still say namaz?'

'Ammi, how did you get bloodstains on your shalwar?' she asks, staring at the stains. There are a few rust-coloured spots of dried blood on the crotch of the white shalwar. 'How did this happen? What did you do?'

Her mother confesses to her deed, fumbling and faltering like a little girl caught in a mischievous act. Ammi is on blood thinners. She was shaving her pubic hair when the razor scraped her skin. Why? Why? Her mother can't hold a pen and sign her name, her hands tremble so much. She can't pour out a glass of water, can't hold a cup of tea. What the hell was she doing with a razor?

She's so furious, she can't trust herself to speak calmly. She has to take several deep breaths and urge herself to be patient, composed. The way she had been when they were returning home from a consultation with the neurologist, when she was grappling with his diagnosis of her mother's condition – Alzheimer's.

'Why were you shaving your pubic hair?' she now asks in a patient, composed voice.

'Won't it keep growing if I don't?' her mother says meekly.

'So what if it grows?'

'How will I say my prayers if I don't shave all that hair?'

'It doesn't say anywhere in the Quran that you can't pray if you don't shave your pubic hair.'

'It's unclean. It's napaak. Don't you shave yours?'

'No.'

'You don't?'

'I don't.'

'When did you stop?'

She is about to say, when I left home. Instead, she replies, 'I stopped when I stopped having my periods.'

She rinses her mother's bloodstained shalwar. She rubs detergent paste on the stains and puts the garment in the laundry basket. Had Ammi kept shaving her pubic hair well past menopause to make herself more sanitized and appealing for her husband? But she can't ask her mother this. The sort of intimacy that comfortably accommodates such questions has never been there between mother and daughter. Her parents have been sleeping in separate rooms for years. That's all she knows.

'I don't want you to do this again, Ammi. Okay? Don't you know what could happen if you get a deeper-than-usual cut? You could bleed to death. No, I'm serious. You'd be bleeding away in the bathroom and nobody would know. So stop this shaving business. There's no need. God doesn't care if you pray with or without your pubic hair.'

She finds her mother a clean shalwar from the closet and helps her change into it.

'When did you stop having your periods?' Ammi asks, sitting on the edge of the bed as she struggles to pull on the shalwar.

She hasn't told her mother about her menopause, the gut-heavy years of depression, the nights of sweating, the lonely hours spent awake.

'It's been a few years.'

'When do men stop?' Ammi asks.

'Stop what? Men don't have periods. What's there to stop?'

'I know they don't have periods but…' Her mother stares into the gathering dusk, looking perplexed and abandoned.

The thought crosses her mind that Ammi wants to talk about her father and her disillusionment with him, but it would be futile to go down that path. There'd be nothing new. She could listen to stories she had already heard, but she doesn't want to. It's better to take Ammi out and wait for the azaan on the verandah. She gets a glimpse of her mother's hesitant face and feels the weight of her oft-repeated tales. She tries to guess at the questions beneath her mother's stale stories: *when do men stop wanting sex? Why do they get tired of their wives? Why do they run after younger women? Do men go through menopause? Has your husband ever been unfaithful to you?*

She sits with her mother in silence, not sure if she has the right words to share her grief. What if she could use more words, different sorts of words? Would her mother feel comforted by the inevitableness of her answers, then? She's saved by the loud and discordant notes of the azaan blaring from several neighbourhood mosques at once. Her mother covers her head with her dupatta. The mosquitoes start droning. Relieved, she helps her mother back over the threshold into the house and walks with her to the bathroom to wait for her as she performs her ablutions.

3

Slut Series

Slut 1

Baba would stop by at her place even before Amma's death. He would tap the back gate with his cane and wait till she came out and placed something in his bowl. After Amma was buried, the remaining summer holidays stretched for several weeks. In the still, breezeless afternoons, the neem trees in the schoolyard stood motionless and the heat made the walls sigh. She would doze off, waiting for the tap of Baba's cane on the cobblestones outside her window. She would place the roti she had saved for him in his bowl. He wouldn't leave immediately. Especially after Amma was no more, he always found time to talk to her. Once, he told her how he had been robbed of whatever he had earned on the very steps of the shop where he usually slept. Then the rains came. The water rose. And it became impossible for him to sleep out in the open.

She asked him if he would like to sleep on the covered verandah outside her room. He didn't need much space. He moved in with his alms bowl, his cane and a jute bag containing two torn kurtas, caps and two dhotis. He settled down on Amma's cot in the verandah. That night, the two pairs of slippers on the doormat, his and hers, eased the heaviness within her. She felt safe sleeping in her little room, knowing he was sleeping outside.

He left early in the morning with his bowl and cane, long before the schoolchildren arrived. When he returned in the evening, he laid before her whatever he had received. It was a strange feeling, sharing the mixed-up food he had collected from different houses, something she had never imagined herself doing. But she overcame her initial distaste. For the first time since Amma's death, she didn't have to eat alone. If he brought enough, she didn't bother cooking. If he didn't bring much, she would light the stove and cook rice. The alms he received, he gave her to keep in a safe place till it was time for him to go to his village.

After the rains, she didn't ask him to move out. Nor did he suggest it. He stayed on. A year passed. Baba asked her to give him his savings, as he was going to the village to see his family for Eid. But before he left for the mosque, the two of them got into an argument.

'I've got you a new kurta and dhoti with my own money,' she told him. 'Not as if I have a lot to spare. At least, on Eid, you should bathe and put on clean clothes.'

'I'm going to the mosque to beg,' he said. 'Who'll give me money if I'm dressed in new clothes? As if to pacify her, he added, 'I'll bathe when I come back.'

'No, why should you? Don't bother. Go straight to your village from the mosque,' she replied irritably and got busy cleaning her room, dusting and sweeping every corner of it. She liked to clean and have everything in order. Dirt disturbed her. Getting used to eating the food he brought back from so many houses had not been easy, but hadn't she done it for his sake?

She bathed and cooked seviyan. She didn't expect him to return from the mosque. He didn't. He left for the village straight from there. She lay down for a nap, woke up, made

tea, said her prayers. In the evening, she changed into her
new shalwar-kurta and went out to visit her neighbours.

—∾—

'You know tongues wag. Not mine. Allah forbid. But the
whole mohalla is talking about you and him. After all, you're
a mature woman. You are expected to guard your izzat.'

'What have I done to my izzat?' Sultana asked, replacing
the spoon in the seviyan bowl.

Suddenly, she had no desire to eat anything served in this
house.

'They're saying you're behaving like...a loose, bazari
woman.'

'I've allowed a homeless fakir to sleep on my verandah.
What's bazari about that?'

'But you're a married woman...'

'I'm not a married woman.'

'Has your husband divorced you?'

'You know I left my husband thirty years ago. Nobody
ever called him bazari for living with another woman right
under my nose.'

As long as Amma was living, nobody would have dared
allude to her as a bazari woman. Walking back home, flustered
and angry, she covered the distance – it was a few yards from
the neighbour's house to the schoolyard – in agitated strides.
She entered her room and shut the only window that opened
out onto the world. Suddenly, the shiny brass utensils and
gifts her mother had given for her wedding swam before her
eyes. All those gifts which her in-laws had refused to return to
her when she left their house. Amma had scraped the bottom
of her savings and borrowed to buy brass trays and bowls.
She had filled them with sweets and dry fruit and silk saris.
Amma had wrapped her in one of those shimmering saris
and sent her along with the gifts to serve a man about whom

all she knew was this: he earned a good living as a driver. The heavy bed and dresser and closet Amma had sent along as wedding gifts required two men to move them up the narrow stairs into that windowless, airless room she was to share for a decade with her driver-husband. Swaddled in silk and gold, barely able to see where she was being taken through the maze of narrow rooms, she had climbed up those stairs with dread.

'Where did I go wrong?' Amma had later asked through a veil of tears. 'I had made all the enquiries before your marriage.'

'Don't cry, Amma,' she said. 'Isn't it better that I came back alive? He would've killed me if he could.'

Was it the shame of a married daughter coming back to her parental home that had killed Amma? Sultana still carried the guilt within her like a morsel stuck in her throat.

—ᴍ—

School reopened after Eid and Sultana went about her chores, carrying out her duties, but hardly speaking to anybody. Every day, she waited to see if Baba would return. She rose early and after namaz, prayed for Baba's safety. She drank tea, then walked across the schoolyard and began her daily chores: dusting and sweeping, fetching, sorting, filing. She was the lady peon for the girls' wing and she was always in demand, sought out by students, teachers – all the staff. If nobody knew where the extra cups and glasses were stored or where the Home Science project materials were kept, Sultana was the only one who could tell them.

But as soon as school was over and the vast courtyard emptied of the loud chattering girls, unwanted thoughts assailed her again. She stared at the desks and benches; they reflected her emptiness back to her. What was she to do with herself? How was she to live till the next day? She started staying up late at night, reciting God's names on her tasbih. Every time she prostrated herself before the invisible, ever-present One, whose presence she never doubted, she pleaded, 'What is the purpose of my life? You are the only One who knows. You are the only One who can save my izzat. Am I a bazari woman?'

After many days had passed, she heard the tap of Baba's cane on the cobblestones. Her clenched jaw slackened, her eyes lost their faraway look, her gait lost its brisk severity and her innards seem to relax and glow, as if she had swallowed a lighted lamp. Baba entered and handed her the sack of rice, jaggery and coconuts he had brought for her from the village, as if he were merely returning from his daily round of begging.

She brought him a glass of water. She pounded ginger and made tea. He sat on the bench in the verandah, sipping his tea slowly, looking pleased. She hurriedly put on a pot of water to boil rice.

'How's your family in the village?' she asked.

'I shouldn't have gone at all. I should've just stayed with you for Eid.'

His sons and their wives and his grandchildren didn't really want him. He said he had felt trapped, stuck and nothing but a hindrance to them.

'They're calling me bazari, these mohallawalas, because of you, Baba. I'm not going to visit them ever again.'

'Do you know what my family would call me if they knew I beg in the city?'

'I don't know. I don't even want to know,' Sultana said, as a tear rolled down her cheek, fell into the simmering pot of rice and disappeared amidst the bubbles. 'I'm just glad you're back. What do I care? Let them talk.'

Slut 2

'You're not to kiss me.'

'Why not?'

'I don't let any customer do it. And no sucking on my tits either.'

'What the fuck am I paying you for, then…?'

'A quick fuck is what you pay me for.'

'So I can't suck your tits?'

'No.'

'What the fuck…'

'There's another one waiting. Hurry up. And put this on.'

'What's this?'

'Condom.'

'What for?'

'For your own good.'

'What the hell do you care about my good?'

'Put it on! Or get out.'

'Saali! I'm not going to pull on any condom-shondom. Who's the boss here? Give me back the hundred I paid. Who do you think you are? I'll fuck you for free. Chal, get up on your knees. Can't do this. Can't do that. What sort of whore are you? Shut up and let me do what I paid you for.'

—⁓—

'Listen! Either you put on this condom or you get out. Here's your hundred. Get out. I don't need your kind. Uncle! Oh Uncle…do you hear me? Come and get this ass out of here.'

'Don't call me an ass. I'm leaving. But what sort of slut are you? Don't you need the money?'

'I'm the slut who's a schoolteacher's daughter.'

'I don't believe you.'

'What don't you believe?'

'That you're a teacher's daughter.'

'My father was the head teacher in the village school.'

'Your father was a teacher? No!…How did you end up here?'

'My father was my first customer. My only customer – till I killed him.'

'You killed your father?'

'I killed my father.'

'What kind of a woman are you?'

'The kind of woman who killed her father. Come on. Get going. The other guy is waiting. Get used to using condoms. It's for your own good.'

—⁓—

'Ay, Uncle! Haven't I told you a thousand times to tell these bastards before you send them in about condoms and kissing? And don't send in the ones that waste so much of my time. They don't care if they get AIDS. Those NGO people come to lecture us. Why don't they tell these bastards about condoms? Where's Rani? Was she crying? Didn't you give her any milk? Rani? My baby!'

She sits on the cot, lifts up her kurta and lets Rani's hungry mouth find her breast. As Rani's little mouth begins to tug at her nipple, she bends down to kiss her almost hairless head.

The last customer of the day was a truck driver who almost crushed her under his bulk. But he didn't protest against the no-kissing rule and didn't fuss about the condom. Her day's earnings amount to only four hundred rupees. But at least, the policeman didn't come round today to ask for his daily share. She'll be able to get chicken for dinner.

Suddenly, Munni bleats for attention, sitting on her haunches in the dirt.

She calls to her. 'Ay, Munni, ay, Munya, come here!'

She holds out grass for Munni, while Rani nurses. Munni

nibbles at the grass and Rani's warm head nestles against her breast. Suddenly, Rani stops suckling. She looks up into her face and smiles her toothless smile.

She addresses Munni and Rani: 'Aren't you two happy? Work is over for Mother. And there's enough money for chicken. Now I will cook.'

Contentment spreads on her face as she stares into the gathering dusk. Tomorrow is still twelve hours away.

Slut 3

Dear Di,

I just wanted to talk to you. I don't know why. I know it's late and I can't call you. So I'm mailing you. I want to come and see you as soon as school opens.

Am wearing these jeans – see the pix – I made slits on both knees. You will be happy to know I didn't slit my knees. And those old cuts on my arms have started healing. See pix. I am sending you all these pix, so you'll believe me when I say I'm not cutting myself any more.

You asked me last time we met if I cut myself because I felt helpless.

I'm not helpless, but I'm not strong either. I can't punch somebody in the face. When I get angry, I want to punch people in the face, but I don't. I'm not strong enough. But I guess I can hurt them with my words. Really hurt with words. And when I scream, I really scream.

Di, why do I keep having dreams like this? I see myself eating a packet of Kurkure and a terrorist walks up to me and shoots me. I can't even jump over the gate to safety. I jump over the gate and land on the wrong side – right into the terrorist's arms! Or I'm walking in my dream and I see a man coming towards me with a big log and he smashes it in my face. It was so real, I could feel the cuts and wounds on my face when I woke up.

I don't want to be here any more. I mean here. In the world. My dad called me a slut (again!), just because I was talking to R late at night. When I was in Class IX, he called me a slut just for having a phone-boyfriend. I hate him. I want to kill him. You know what he said? He said, 'Go have sex with your BF if you want to; just don't come back home with AIDS.'

I yelled at him. I said, 'Dad, I'm not a slut just for talking to a guy on the phone.'

I have this other dream again and again…about the guy who did it to me… He's there and my father's there too… with his good friend… And they're all doing it to me. They're carving 'SLUT' on my stomach with a blade. And my best friend is just standing there, just watching. He's smiling. He does nothing to save me. I got so disturbed after this dream, you know what I did? I went and took off all my clothes in front of R… My best friend. R's hands are like that man's… dark, big. And when I imagine those hands on me down there… I feel sick. I feel like R can't protect me. Nobody can.

I was walking towards the shop near our house…and again, I got this feeling. The icky feeling. I felt sore down there, really sore. I saw his big brown hands down there. I started crying… I used to let him do it, because he would say, 'If you don't let me do what I want to, then I'll do it with your sister; I'll do it with your mother.' And you know what? I found out that he was doing it to my sister and telling her the same thing!

Di, I can't study for my exams. Dad says, 'It's not like you're studying PCM…you're only studying Fine Arts.' He makes me feel like I'm the stupidest girl in the world. I want to dance and paint, instead of studying. I feel like I'm no good at anything. The history teacher made me feel I was the dumbest person in class. She looked at me like this… She even makes faces at me. I don't meet her expectations, even though in the last class, I was the only one to answer all her questions, because nobody else had done the reading.

But something good has happened. My mother and I are better friends now, after I told her what you told me to tell her. But I told her in a horrible way… I said, 'You've always been a horrible mother.' She was hitting me…because we got into an argument and I had answered her back. After her ninth slap, I just exploded. I said, 'Listen, Mom. Where were you when I was raped? I was ten years old. Where were you then?'

She stopped hitting me, but do you know what she did? She started asking me ridiculous questions: 'What did he do to you? Did he make you do this? Did he ask you to do that?'

She doesn't get it. She still doesn't believe it happened to me! She asked, 'Do you even know what rape means?'

As if I don't know what rape means! I told her everything, I was crying, crying… And then she finally hugged me. She said she was sorry she wasn't there for me. We are better friends now.

But it's not much fun being home, Di, and I can't wait to get back to school. Mom and Dad are always fighting. I have to tell you this… I fell ill because of their fights…and I wanted to talk to you because of this, really. Dad is having some sort of affair with Mom's best friend. But he denies it… I showed him her messages on his phone. He just said, 'Oh, what message? I didn't read any message from her.'

'Of course, you didn't read it, Dad, or you would have deleted it!' I said.

I want to tell Dad a lot of things, but I don't. What's the point?

But you know, I felt really sick when Ma started pleading with him. 'You won't do this again, na? You won't, na?'

'Don't apologize, Ma!' I begged her.

The only time I felt happy was when Mom stood up to him and said, 'If you don't leave her, I'll leave you.'

But later, he told her, 'If you don't apologize to me, I'll divorce you.'

Suddenly, she went all meek and started begging him. You don't know my dad, Di; he's so handsome and so manipulative. All the women love him, including Ma.

Ma apologized to him – can you believe it? She apologized!

I told her if I were her, I would rather die than apologize to my husband for having an affair with my best friend.

I better shut up, Di. You'll get sick of reading such a long mail. Sorry, Di, but I had to tell somebody.

4

A Stitch in Time

Amrita called at 6 a.m. This wasn't like her.

'What's up?' I mumbled into the phone.

All I heard were stifled sobs.

'Is everything okay?'

'Can you please meet me for lunch?' she said, after a long pause.

'Yes, but is everything okay?'

I hoped she wouldn't have really bad news to share. I had been up most of the night with my two-year-old's clogged nose and ear infection. I felt incapable of shoring up anybody else's grief after a night like that.

'No. That's why we have to meet,' she replied. 'Come to the shop at noon.'

Amrita ran an alterations-and-darning business downtown. She and I had become friends at a Diwali party which she attended with her husband and children and her turbaned father-in-law whom everybody in the family called Grandpa. One morning, I had visited her at A Stitch in Time, situated on the top floor of an oversize women's clothing store. Amrita had no customers at that time; so she made me coffee and we chatted. The newly opened outlet mall, she said, had diverted the attention of her usual customers away from her store.

After her call that morning, I hauled my unwilling body out of bed. I concealed my fatigue by carrying out my daily chores with more resignation than I did on other days. I made coffee, packed my husband's lunch and my daughter's, put my daughter down for a nap and while she was asleep, sorted out the laundry into light and dark piles, and loaded last night's dinner dishes into the dishwasher.

My daughter's antibiotic was working; she wasn't coughing or throwing up. So I dropped her off at her babysitter's and picked up Amrita. We drove to her favourite place for lunch, Los Nortenos. On Wednesdays, they had their enchilada special, beans and rice, with free refills of iced tea – the whole deal for $3.25.

Amy, from the oversize-clothing department, called out. 'Heading for Los Nortenos?'

Amrita nodded. 'They have their enchilada special!'

'But you shouldn't eat that stuff. Get the taco salad and don't order the tortilla chips. They fry 'em.'

'Okay! I'll only have the taco salad,' Amrita promised in her schoolgirlish, aiming-to-please voice.

In the car, she sighed. 'Amy means well. I told her I want to lose a hundred pounds. "You can't do it without discipline," she said. She used to be a Size Sixteen and in six months, she's down to a Size Twelve. "You can do it too, but you need discipline," she says. She's given me all her Size Sixteen skirts to alter. Ten baked, not fried, chips is her allowance and she never will touch the eleventh chip. That's how you get down to twelve from sixteen in six months. Who's that disciplined?'

—∞—

At Los Nortenos, the Mexican owner greeted us with a broad smile. He had thick, black greased, slicked-back hair and knew he was a hit with the ladies. As soon as we were seated, he told the waitress to bring us the ochre plastic glasses filled with iced tea.

'Ladies, will it be the special?' he asked, smiling his winning smile.

'Yes. It'll be the special,' Amrita said. And forgetting Amy's advice, she added an order of tortilla chips and salsa.

Then she announced the bad news. 'My best friend died.'

'Your best friend?' I murmured.

'My best friend.'

'When? Where?' This was the first time I was hearing about a best friend. 'How old was she?'

'He.'

'Sorry. How old was he?'

'About my age. A little older. He lived in Rwanda. His sister called me. That's when I called you.' 'Rwanda?'

I'd heard about Rwanda on radio and TV. It was a war-torn country in Africa, with a bloody civil war going on. That Amrita's best friend lived in Rwanda seemed far-fetched to me. It seemed too disconnected from her neat, white house, her well-mowed front lawn, her safely tucked away downtown business and our red chequered tablecloth-covered table at Los Nortenos, where we sat with misty glasses of iced tea in our small, safe Texan town.

'How did he die?'

'Pneumonia. He was stuck at his farm because of the war. He did try to fly out to Nairobi, but there were no flights leaving.'

'And what about his family? He had a family, right?'

'He had sent his wife and daughter away to London as soon as the war started.'

'It must be devastating to get that sort of news first thing in the morning,' I said, not really sure what else I could say in that moment.

I had finished my enchiladas and was making furrows

with my fork in the uneaten refried beans. Amrita ate in a dazed and disinterested way and kept dabbing her eyes with a tissue. A pile of used tissues was collecting beside her plate.

For a while, I matched her silence with mine. I felt what she wanted was for me to listen without interrupting her. When she did start talking, she didn't talk about her friend's death. She talked about her father-in-law, instead. She described Grandpa's daily routine, which I'd already heard about during several of our earlier conversations.

'Grandpa woke up at three a.m. today. I heard him in the bathroom, because I was also up. Nothing changes. It's like clockwork. If he's bathing, it must be four. If he's meditating, it must be five. If he's going out the front door, it must be six. When he eats breakfast, it's eight. If he's watering the lawn, it must be five p.m. Reads his holy books at four. Has his tea. Goes out for another walk. Eats dinner. And when he goes to bed, it's eight p.m. Nothing changes in his life. Or mine.'

'Do you want it to?'

She didn't answer my question. 'Do you know how much Grandpa walks?' she said, instead. 'Seven miles! He walks seven miles every day. Winter or summer, rain or snow, he walks seven miles every day.'

Grandpa was a sturdy, simple, upright-as-a pole Sikh. I met him often on my morning walks in our neighbourhood park and he always mumbled something in Punjabi to me. Amrita's husband had asked him to come over to the States after his wife passed away and there was nobody to look after him in India.

'He's older than eighty, Harry thinks.' Amrita's lower lip quivered as she wiped the corners of her eyes. 'My friend... my friend was only forty. Do you know when Grandpa first arrived, I used to make him aloo parathas for breakfast and sabzi roti for lunch, before I left for work. Then I switched him to oatmeal and bananas, because I couldn't be bothered to make the parathas. He didn't complain. He never complains. He eats whatever I give him. But today, I left him oatmeal for lunch as well.'

'It's okay,' I said to soothe Amrita's guilt. 'He can handle oatmeal twice a day once in a while.'

Amrita was going on about Grandpa. 'I don't mind serving him. He's an old man. But when I think of him as Harry's father, I hate him. I want him to leave. But he doesn't want to go back. He likes it here. America is so clean, he says. And safe. He likes the clean sidewalks and parks. There are no sidewalks in Patiala, he says.'

How many times did I have to listen to Amrita complain about her father-in-law? But then, could I blame her? I was just as trapped in the repetitive, unrewarding warp and weft of my own life.

I sensed that Amrita wanted to talk about her friend, but she didn't know how to take the conversation there.

'Seems like you were really close to this friend,' I said, by way of offering an opening.

'I spent my childhood with him. His sister was my classmate. The three of us played together.'

'You liked him?'

Amrita looked away. 'Yes, a lot. But I couldn't marry him. He was a Hindu and he was younger than me.'

'So?'

'So you know how it is. Dad said to me, "Amrita, you'll say, 'Sat-sari-akaal' and he will say, 'Ram Ram.' What will your children say?" As soon as I graduated from high school, Dad flew me to Chandigarh in the middle of this really awful summer. He advertised for a groom in the newspapers. Harbhajan answered the ad. He came with his father and took one look at me and said yes. He and his father went out and when they came back, they had brought boxes of sweets to announce our engagement. He was very

happy that he could come and live in America.' Amrita's
tone was flat, distant.

'And then?'

'Then nothing. We had a big wedding in Chandigarh and
came back here. He got his US visa and ticket from us. Then
just before I turned twenty, Mandeep was born.'

'When did Harbhajan become Harry?'

'After he came here. He said we have to learn from the
Chinese. They all adopt American names.'

'And your friend?'

'He waited for me. But after a few years, he gave up. He
moved to Rwanda. Ugh… I forgot to take my Xanax today.'
Amrita rummaged in her purse.

'And you stayed on with Harry.'

'What else could I do? I had Mandeep. Harry's a habit
now. A bad habit.'

'Does the Xanax help?'

Amrita clicked the lid back into place after removing a
pill. 'Without it, I wouldn't be able to get out of bed in the
mornings. You should try it. Makes you feel calm and clear-
headed.'

'Give me some to take with me. I'll need it in India!' I said.

'Can you do me a favour? Can Grandpa go back to India
with you? He's afraid to travel alone.'

'Why not? If you can get him a ticket on the same flight.'

—⁂—

It was Thanksgiving and I was at Amrita's with my daughter.
My husband had taken off to spend the long weekend with
his old college friends who were all gathering in Tennessee.
Our apartment was a mess, but he had gone. Shouldn't he
have stayed behind to help? Wasn't this supposed to be a
fifty-fifty deal? There were mover's boxes, books, unfolded
laundry and piles of unsorted mail. My mind swirled amidst

vague, troubling notions of how to become more organized, more efficient and more patient with my two-year-old, while trying to sort out and pack our belongings into boxes that had to be shipped. I didn't have the courage to admit to myself that my marriage was as chaotic as the mess that surrounded me in the apartment.

Amrita's brother and sister-in-law were visiting from Detroit for Thanksgiving. Another Indian couple – a psychiatrist and his wife – were the other guests.

I was helping Amrita fry the pakoras. The November afternoon was fading fast outside her kitchen window. It reminded me of what I thought my life would be like in India. I felt anxiety bubble up from my stomach and spread out like heartburn over my chest. Xanax would be good. I was on the verge of asking Amrita for it. I had no idea what small-town life in India would be like. Would it be similar to small-town life in the USA? Would it be like what it was here? Like this?

The bare, brown November trees stoodstark and still against a low, brooding sky. The oil sizzled in the karhai as I dropped the blobs of pakora batter into it. The hospitable disorder of Amrita's kitchen and the warm aromas wafting from her oven steadied me. There was something maternal, comforting about food. While the pakoras were frying, I gazed out at the sidewalk beyond the stretch of Amrita's scrubby lawn, where the breeze scattered the weightless brown leaves. But here, in the kitchen, all was solid, warm, safe.

'I marinate my turkey in ginger-garlic and yogurt paste,' Amrita declared with a rare show of pride. 'Makes it very tender.'She pulled out the shelf to check on the twenty-pound turkey in the oven.

Amrita's daughter, Mandy, walked in to take Grandpa's tray to his room. Grandpa didn't eat turkey; he was a vegetarian. He had to go to bed by eight and we would behaving dinner only after the men had finished several rounds of whiskey and pakoras.

Amrita's marinade had worked wonders. It had given the turkey a sweet, chewy moistness. Every mouthful of meat, coated with thick, garlicky gravy, and the creamy mashed potatoes and beans seemed to instil in me a sense of tranquillity and forgetfulness. Pumpkin chiffon pie and cardamom chai took forgetfulness to an even higher dimension. My anxieties about my future move faded away as we talked about how much we had eaten and collapsed on the couches in the living room.

Harry was playing on the new computer with his two sons, Mandy's younger brothers. His latest purchase had been a really good deal from Best Buy and that was all he talked about over dinner. Amrita's brother and the psychiatrist poured out more whiskey. And we, the women, moved back to the kitchen after a few minutes' rest to put away leftovers and do the dishes.

'Let me help you.' Amrita's brother had entered the kitchen and was addressing me, picking up a dishcloth. He had said very little to Amrita all evening. It made me wonder what sort of relationship brother and sister shared.

'I hear you're moving back to India?' he asked me.

'Yes.'

'I guarantee you'll be back in a year,' he said with the sort of certitude I could never muster about my life and certainly not with a stranger.

'You're trying to scare me!'

'No, I'm serious. You'll see for yourself. On your husband's government salary, you'll barely manage to survive. You won't be able to buy a car. Or an AC. Until we left India, our parents couldn't afford an AC or a fridge or a TV. Nothing like this.' He waved a hand at the electronics cornucopia strewn around Amrita's living room.

It was at this point that Amrita's sister-in-law came to my rescue and changed the topic of conversation from electronics to turkeys. 'Bhabiji,' she said to her sister-in-law, 'yours was the best turkey I've ever had. Do you add garlic to the gravy too?'

Amrita smiled her grateful, schoolgirl smile. 'Lots of it. Garlic is good for cholesterol.'

'Should I tell you what I dream of?' her brother said to me. He had paused, stopped drying the dishes and picked up his glass from the counter. 'My dream is to own an Indian restaurant and eat pakoras and samosas made in my own restaurant.'

—∞—

Some days later, Amrita called, sounding tearful again. She'd had an argument with Harry. About Grandpa. One of her relatives was going to India and she had suggested Grandpa go back with them. But Harry didn't think it was appropriate to ask Grandpa to leave, since the old man didn't seem ready to go. Amrita then asked Grandpa if he would like to go back to India with us. Harry had got mad at her for asking him.

It was at the tail end of a fast-vanishing, cold December afternoon that I entered Amrita's house. Outside, it was already quite dark, but Amrita's kitchen was bright and untidy. My daughter started playing with Mandy and soon fell asleep on their living-room couch. Mandy joined us for chai. She was a high-school senior, big-boned like her mother, broad-faced like her father, with a perpetually cheery attitude which gave the impression that she was trying to cover up parts of herself she didn't want to show the world.

'Mom!' Mandy said, 'are you asking Grandpa to leave?'

'Mandeep, I didn't ask him to leave,' Amrita replied. She was the only one who insisted on calling Mandy by her birth name. 'All I said was he could go back and meet his relatives for a couple of months. Then he could come back. That's all.'

'So why is Dad in such a funk? I don't get it.'

'I don't know, Mandeep, why your Dad is in a bad mood.'

'Neither you nor Dad sound like yourselves these days.'

I stepped in to avert an argument. 'Mandy, do you know your mom lost a close friend recently?'

'She did? Mom, how come you never tell me anything that's going on in your life.'

'When should I tell you? When do you have the time to listen to me? Anyway, you didn't know him. He lived in Rwanda.'

'Is that in Africa? I think I recall that from my Geography class.'

'Yes.'

'Wow, Mom! I didn't know you had friends in Africa! In such far-off places! How did he die?'

'Pneumonia.'

'Don't they have doctors and hospitals in Rwanda?'

'There's a war going on in Rwanda. He couldn't get to the hospital in time.'

Amrita was staring out of her kitchen window at the sidewalk, just the way I had been staring out of that same window at the same sidewalk a couple of weeks back.

Mandy noticed her mother's absent look and started telling me about the rock concert she had recently attended in Houston. 'You should've seen the dresses some of the older women were wearing. Some of them were old! I mean, *old*. Like fifties or sixties. There was this one woman in a black dress with a slit all the way up to here!' Mandy traced a finger from her ankles to her hips. 'I mean, she was nasty-looking. Nasty, nasty legs…'

Amrita snapped, 'You shouldn't talk like that, Mandeep. About other people.'

'I guess I can never say or do anything right. Right, Mom? Especially, when you're in one of your moods.' Mandy stormed out. Then re-entered, backpack on shoulder. 'I'll be at Jim's place, working on my term paper. Don't wait up for me at dinner.'

'Maybe, it's good you're moving to India. Look how Mandeep talks to me,' Amrita said, as if speaking to someone or something beyond the kitchen window. 'Your daughter will grow up nicely in India.'

—∞—

We're leaving for India, but Grandpa isn't going with us. Not with us and not with Amrita's relative. He's not going anywhere. He's staying in his son's house. Amrita invites us to a farewell dinner. All evening, she's quieter than usual.

Just as we are leaving, I go into the kitchen and ask, 'Are you okay, Amrita? You don't seem yourself.'

She looks at me with the resigned expression of someone who has mastered the noble art of accepting the intolerable. 'I wanted him to leave. But I'm okay. He doesn't want to go.'

—∞—

I have a fight with my husband. About his absences, about him not helping out. Why can't he clear up all the mess lying on the living-room floor? Why can't he help me clean and pack? He's doing his best, he says, and can't do much more. I stand against the kitchen sink and wonder for the thousandth time why I'm still with him if life is so intolerable. PMS? Yes, it could be. I hope it is. I tend to get very irritable just before my periods. Hopefully, I'll feel better next week when my periods are over. I hang on to that hope.

'Mamma crying? Mamma crying?' My daughter waddles into the kitchen, holding her frayed blankie in one hand and her thumb in her mouth.

'No, Mamma's not crying. Mamma will take you to the park, okay? After she packs two more boxes. You want all your toys in India, don't you?'

There's freshly brewing anxiety in my gut about this move. I wish I could vomit out all this anxiety. Something has to redeem me. When I'm like this, I'm really capable of doing anything, walking out. Leaving everything just as it is and walking out. But I usually have a good cry and calm down. The anxiety settles and I go on doing whatever it was I was doing before.

I sit in the car after I bring my daughter back from the park. She has fallen asleep in her car seat. I feel unable to get out of the car and carry her the short distance to our apartment. Beyond the windshield, a big pot-bellied man is riding the mower. There's the uncut grass and the unruffled greyness of a woolly sky and the brownness of naked trees and brown fences. Where would I be safe? *Right here, right here*, my heart thuds, and I go back to watching the man go round and round in circles on the mower, dividing the lawn into cut and uncut circles of grass. Later in the evening, I drive out to the laundromat and watch blankets and sleeping bags whirl in the extra-large industrial-size washer. They have to be washed before I pack them into boxes. I go into a trance, unable to take my eyes off the washer.

5

Panjpir Chowk

Friday, March 5, 2009: the mausoleum of the 17th-century Sufi poet Rahman Baba was bombed by militants. The horrible incident is still fresh in the minds of Baba's followers, and visitors continue to feel reluctant to pay their respects at the resting place of their favourite Sufi poet. Rahman Baba (1653–1711) is considered the undisputed Pashto bard... The shrine of Baba, once an abode of peace and spiritual solace, could never be the same again for devotees and visitors after the bombing.... Located in the rural Hazarkhwani area on the outskirts of Peshawar, a broken and bumpy road leads to the shrine of the Sufi poet, where before the militants' attack 1,500 people showed up every day. But now, it has dismally trickled down to around 300 daily visitors.... Taleban leaders have said in the past that they are opposed to women visiting shrines because they believe it promotes obscenity. Residents of Hazarkhwani area on the eastern outskirts of Peshawar – where the shrine of Rahman Baba is located – say that local Taleban groups had warned that if the women continued to visit the shrine, they would blow it up.

You haven't given much thought to visiting the shrines of Sufi saints, though you read Sufi poetry and you love Rumi. But because she, the life of your universe, your jaan-e-jahaan, wants to visit the shrine of the five saints, you say yes. You conceal your hair under a drab cotton chadar that you hope renders you unremarkable. As you're getting into the cab, you notice she hasn't covered her head. She never does and you worry – if we're going out in public, shouldn't she? She's the one living in Taleban country; she must know what she's doing. Risk and resistance – you know her arguments too well; so you stay quiet.

The cab driver is a typical northern-areas man, with a reddish face and thick beard, like most men in this town. A soft, grey rain starts to fall as the cab merges with the traffic on the main street leading into the old town.

'Panjpir Chowk,' she tells the driver.

'Panjpir shrine in Old City?' the man clarifies.

'Yes.'

'You want to go to the shrine at Panjpir?' he asks again, as if he hadn't heard right, as if he's surprised that we would want to go there.

It's a cool, lazy afternoon, made cooler by the rain. Gone is the heat of the day. Dense grey clouds veil the mountains at the rim of the town. These are the same mountains you gaze at from her living-room window. Most mornings, you watch them in silence, while listening to the sounds drifting up from the lane below. You gaze at forlorn clouds wandering across the sky from the gaps between houses. Your days are about solitude and slowness.

You are secluded from outsiders by the high-walled balcony and like most women in town, you listen without speaking or being seen: to footsteps of passers-by, the vegetable sellers, the knife sharpener, squealing schoolboys, men's voices talking on their mobiles. You hear, but don't see them. They neither hear nor see you.

Then she gets back from work. There's music and tea. Life returns to the apartment with her.

'Not too loud – we don't want to attract the attention of the neighbours,' she warns you when you turn up the volume on a qawwali.

'It's only a qawwali. We're not partying!'

'The neighbours are wary about me, suspicious. I'm a single woman. A working woman. They're not used to women like us.'

'Aren't you being a bit too cautious?'

'I live here. I know.'

'But you go out without covering your head!'

'Some risks I take. Some, I don't.'

'Why is music more of a risk than covering your head?'

Questions. Questions. Some days, you are restless with an unnamed anxiety about her existence in this place full of questions, where the very existence of an independent woman is a question mark. The mountains remain mute; no matter how much you stare at them, they never offer answers. You need movement to quell your restlessness; so you dust and put away her books and take long showers till the hot water runs out; you wash clothes and hang them out to dry. In the late afternoon, you lean back against the high wall of the balcony, tired of questions you never stop asking about the whys and hows of a woman's life.

Exhausted, you collect the washed clothes, dried and stiffened by the sun, all your days sequestered from life passing in the lane below.

When the sun departs, leaving the balcony dark and cold, sometimes, after dinner, the two of you, wrapped in shawls, sit and watch the stars and the moon from the balcony. Slowness is bestowed by limitations; and seclusion is a limitation, a surprise among the many unasked-for surprises you have received in coming here. And just as you are becoming accustomed to its rhythms, it's time to return.

—⚹—

Panjpir shrine is located in the old part of town. Outside the shrine's entrance, a bearded man is selling birdseed for feeding pigeons. His eyes follow you – two city women who, it seems to him, from the way you walk, are outsiders. She finally covers her head with her chadar, before stepping inside through the green doorway.

Inside, the silence and intimacy and sacredness of the cloister-like courtyard is like a womb. No wonder shrines are visited by forlorn lovers and seekers. Silence is the only container deep enough to hold love's suffering. You wait in the soft green shadow of a walnut tree and she steps into the inner sanctum with the tombs of the five saints. You notice another grave, a tiny one, a child's, in a corner of the courtyard. You read the poetry on its marble gravestone. The child was not even a year old at the time of death:

Phool to do din bahar-e-jaanfiza dikhla gaye
Hairat un ghunchon pe hai jo bin khile murjha gaye.
Flowers bloomed and dazzled with their brief beauty
But alas, the buds that withered without blossoming.

You imagine the parents of the child overcoming their grief by focussing on tangibles, choosing the appropriate stone and couplet for engraving, making sure the words were carved just right.

The birds grow restless and chattier as the afternoon deepens. A hesitant rain stops and starts again. You sit on a low wall in the shelter of the walnut tree, waiting for her, gratefully inhaling the rain-filled silence. In a niche in the wall sits a blackened lamp holder with clay diyas, most of them burnt down; but a few wicks are still burning. Lamps are lit by visitors as they arrive. Do they come here and light lamps, driven by unanswered love, burdened by dashed hopes, struggling to give vent to that which only dead saints can give ear to?

Two women have tiptoed in, holding incense sticks, their

heads covered and faces partially veiled by chadars. They could be friends, lovers, sisters. Ora mother and daughter. The older woman is the stouter one. The slender young one lights incense sticks from a burning lamp and wedges them into crevices in the latticework wall. The two of them whisper, then cease talking and stand motionless. Hands folded, they recite silent prayers, only their lips moving. When they finish praying, they turn to look at you. You sense the ongoing guesswork in their eyes. Then they leave as noiselessly as they had entered.

You walk over to the entrance of the inner sanctum and peep in. It takes a few moments for your eyes to get accustomed to the gloom. There are five raised tombs, draped with green and gold chadars, rose petals strewn on each. And then you see her standing in a corner by one of them. She looks ghostly in the faint, filigreed light from the latticework jali. She seems lost to the world, eyes closed, head bent. You step out, because a man stares at you as you try to stand close to her. You retrace your steps back to the tree, away from his inquisitive eyes.

When she finally emerges, there's the serenity and solidity of mountains about her and yet she appears sweet and defenceless. You want to gather her in your arms. You have the sudden urge to do something motherly, something that would utterly simplify life's many enigmas. You could go out begging for alms and the two of you could just live on what you received. You mention this to her.

'What's come over you?' she almost chuckles. 'What sort of talk is this?'

Later, you wonder what came over you. How did the sensual and maternal morph so seamlessly in you? It doesn't make sense. In the courtyard of the five saints, imagining yourself as a beggar with a begging bowl seemed such a natural thing.

The two of you rest on the low wall under the walnut tree.

'It's nice that they don't stop women from going in to pray,' you say, after a long silence.

'Don't be surprised if that changes soon,' she warns. 'Left to the T, they'll outlaw women from shrines altogether. They have already declared praying at shrines un-Islamic.'

'The T? You mean the Taleban?'

'Shh! Not so loud. Even the walls have ears! If they could blow up Rahman Baba's shrine, couldn't they bomb this one too?'

'I think they are only interested in bombing the famous shrines. Whatever gets them into the news.'

Just then, a hunched beggar enters and limps up to you. His right hand is outstretched. His eyes are downcast. You realize he's not a local, because he's not bothered that you're not locals. He carries the unmistakable non-belongingness of a migrant. You place a ten-rupee note in his hand and watch his fingers close over it. His childlike smile widens as he retreats deferentially.

The courtyard begins to fill with more devotees. The shrine begins to hum with movement: people pray, walk, light lamps and incense. You sense questioning gazes and though nobody says anything to you, you feel it's better to leave. Out on the street, the constant scrutiny of passers-by doesn't end. Something in you turns defiant.

'Let's have tea,' you say, feeling the need to assert yourself in simple ways.

You walk over confidently to a tea stall adjacent to the shrine's entrance and speak to the owner.

'Can we get qahwa? And two chairs?'

The baffled man, who's not used to women customers, fishes out two dirty plastic chairs from the back of his shack. The shop boy dusts them. And places them under the awning. In a few minutes, two steaming cups of sweet, green cardamom-flavoured qahwa appear. It's drizzling again and you wonder if either of you will recall, several years later, a single moment of this afternoon of rain and tea at a tea shack outside the five saints' shrine.

A car pulls up next to the shrine. A prosperous-looking woman, wrapped like cargo in an embroidered chadar, emerges from the back, two men armed with rifles holding the door open for her. Her eyes, two furtive lamps, dart out from the non-veiled space of her face. Envious, she's envious of us, you think. Or maybe, she's afraid of you two – two women sitting out in the street, drinking tea. Daring to do the most ordinary thing.

The beggar comes up to you again. You wonder if he's going to ask for more money. Instead, he waves a charred corn cob at you, nodding vigorously. When you accept his offering, he smiles. You break the corn cob into two and return one half to him.

'Crazy Pathan, chalyahan se!' the tea-shop owner scolds him.

The beggar limps back to his perch on a boulder across the street.

You bite into the salty, burnt corn and sip the sweet qahwa. Salt mingles with sweetness in an uplifting way.

'Isn't this a nice gift,' you say, chewing on the corn. 'He's the only one who seems completely unaware of our presence as something out of the ordinary here.'

The beggar has intensified your longing to become a beggar yourself. What would it be like to be free of fears, even if you had to beg for your daily bread? You save his cob in your purse as a reminder of this strange meeting. His face is a story of suffering and separation, but it carries hope, the kind of hope only the utterly simple or the mad can carry. It is not a brutalized face. You can see from his eyes that he has not yet become embittered.

—∞—

By the time you get home, it has stopped raining. The evening grows chilly. She gets up on a chair to close the roshandaan. You are falling in love with a lot here – qahwa, corn, the mountains, the impossible-to-predict mountain weather. Their loss will hit you hard when you get back to your uncaring city life, to its unceasing chaos and monotony.

You make tea and settle down on the mattress under the warmth of the razai. She puts on music. Abida's voice lights up the evening:

> *Aql ke madrase se uth, ishq ke maikade me aa*
> *Jaam-e-fana o bekhudi ab to piya jo ho so ho**

'That beggar was like a true fakir, a sage,' I murmur.

'Why do you say that?'

'Because he had to have quit the madrasa of rationalityto live like he lives. He was in some other space I can't ever access. Did you notice how foolish and wise he looked when he offered me the corn? I want to be like him. That's not rational, is it?'

'No, my darling! But revelations about the self aren't often rational! How you felt was how you felt. Accept it. You've been educated far too long. All that education gets in the way. But you'll know when the time is right to lose yourself and become a fakir,' she whispers, taking away your cup, bending down, brushing your lips with hers.

You push her away. No, you can't do it. Imagine yourself, a city woman, giving up your job and life and becoming a beggar with a bowl! Just because a sweet beggar man appeared at a shrine. You start dreaming, wanting to go out begging like him, to live like a fakir. You know you won't do it.

---

* Those who leave the school of rationality can enter the tavern of Love Drink the blissful wine of Love and perish with ecstasy.

You didn't even want to go to the shrine. And you come back with this strange longing!

She is sitting next to you on the mattress that serves as her bed and sofa and leans her head against your shoulder. 'You received what you were meant to receive at the shrine. You'll do whatever you're meant to do. Trust yourself. The entire universe is a movement of love and we're part of that movement,' she says.

'And what about all the worldly movements? Jobs and survival and all that? Success and failure?'

'My well-educated lady, those are but surface things. They seem real and they rule our lives. We pay most attention to them. But love is the primary thing and the world is nothing but the potting soil in which to grow love. The soil is made up of the Taleban and Americans, politics and terrorism and war and suffering. That's the soil in which our love has to lay down its roots.'

She fetches a thick book, a translation of Rahman Baba's poetry, a volume you realize you had dusted earlier in the day.

'Look what Rahman Babasays about the beloved. It doesn't matter if the beloved is male or female. Human or divine. He lived in a difficult time. A time like ours, but he paid no heed to the rulers. He couldn't care about Aurangzeb's machinations. He made poetry, instead.'

'What if the beloved is neither male nor female? Like both or in-between or beyond? I don't know what I mean.'

'You don't know what you mean? Or you don't want to know? You know who you are, but you don't see how you've squeezed yourself into one or the other of the moulds on offer? Male or female. Love needs no labels! Lovers come in all forms and every in-between form is welcome. Listen:

> I'm so intoxicated with the wine of your lips
> That none could get as drunk as me.

I grasp the petal of your love
As a drowning man clutches at a straw.

Is that a pink stain on your pale cheek,
Or scarlet drops of my own blood?
My tears of anguish just enflame you more,
Like drops of hot fat on the fire.

Love is no fantasy between us,
But the high tide of passion.
The arch of your eyebrows
Draws me in to worship.
Let slip the veil from your face,
Which beams as radiant as the sun.

"Beloved" is not the title I dreamt up –
But God is the one who named you thus
Every feature of your face
Becomes the mark of holy writ.'

She stops reading. 'Love is no fantasy, you see. It is the highest form of worship.'

'Don't stop. Read more.'

'Okay, pyaari. Are you listening with all your heart? This one is called "Nothing Else".

Morning and evening seem the same to those
Who long for you all day long.

All other speech makes no impression on the heart
Of those who have heard your sweet voice.

He forgets all other intoxication
Who drinks the wine of your bowl.

I, Rahman, send prayers and greetings
To whoever brings your greetings to me.'

You sink deeper under the razai and she reads on until your eyelids grow heavy. You've crossed over into another world. Your existence until you met her was merely the kind most bodies with harried minds go through. You had a body and mind that moved and functioned within the limits defined for you.

This poetry reading is no ordinary reading. You are witnessing your own rebirth. You are bewildered at the miracle unfolding through your fast-dissolving self, as the words and the touch of her skin against yours send you into some hazy, nebulous world. Submerged in love-making and poetry, you enter this universe, a beautiful universe, where the anxieties and questions pulling you down can't exert much hold.

Before falling asleep, you remember muttering, 'With such love and beauty, why do I pay so much attention to the terrorists and the Americans and the Taleban, petty men playing petty power games? If only they could taste the intoxication of love like Rahman Baba did, they'd kill less and love more.'

—∞—

It's still dark when you are awakened by the violence of what seems like an explosion. Earthquake? You remember you are in an earthquake-prone area. And then a guttural, hovering noise like the buzzing of a giant insect lasts several minutes. You nestle closer to her. You wait in the darkness for more sounds to rule out what you just heard as part of a dream. But aside from her warmth and steady breathing, the dark room and your own fast-beating heart and the sturdy ticking of the wall clock, nothing defines the reality of that moment. You huddle closer to her and hold her and wait and wait, until sleep finally overcomes you.

—∞—

It's early morning, judging by the dim, greyish light filling the living room. Somebody is clanging the door knocker. There must be a power outage if the person is not ringing the bell.

It's the landlord, you realize, when you reach the door and the man on the other side speaks. He lives a few houses away.

'Salaam, sister. I just wanted to tell you ladies not to go out today. Madam's phone not working?'

'She may have put it on "Silent". Why? Has anything happened?' you ask, bewildered by his sudden visit. You don't open the gate and invite him in. You're not dressed right; nor is your head covered.

'Osama bin Laden was killed. Haven't you watched the news on TV?'

'Osama? No! Who killed him?' you say, recalling that explosion, that giant insect noise in the night.

'The Americans. Or the army. Or both. Who knows, except Allah? Did you know he was hiding in this town?'

'He was living here? In this town?'

'Yes, he was in hiding here for years. Nobody knew. I wouldn't go out today if I were you. May not be safe.'

'We will stay in. Thanks.'

'Allah hafiz.'

You stand, stunned, listening to the landlord's heavy footsteps recede down the concrete steps leading out to the unpaved lane. You hear his feet crunching over the lane's gravel, his footsteps echoing off the walls of the still-unawakened houses.

When you re-enter the living room, you turn on the TV. But there's no electricity.

'Wake up! Wake up!' you tell her.

'I am awake!' she replies in a sleep-heavy voice.

'Did you hear the landlord? Osama was killed. It'll be all over the news now! We will always be in the news for all the wrong reasons. The most wanted terrorist on Uncle Sam's list! And we didn't have an inkling he was hiding in our town! He could've been our neighbour! I heard an explosion in the night. Maybe, they blew up his hideout or something?'

'Maybe. We won't get all the news until the electricity comes back. But in the meantime, why can't we celebrate? We have been gifted another day off. Let's make French toast and coffee!'

'Why did they kill him? Will they leave us alone now?'

'Who? The Taleban? Or the Americans? No, dear, no one will leave anyone alone. Not for a long time yet. And who is "us"? Us women? All the people of this wretched country? Or the people of the world?'

'I don't know. Everybody. I'm just worried.'

'Worrying won't change a thing! Focus on the immediate. We have an extra day of seclusion. Extra space to be what we are and can't be. Are we going to waste it worrying? Do we have eggs for French toast? Let's be extravagant and have that American coffee I got as a gift!'

Unsettled by her cheeriness, you can't ward off your gut-heavy anxiety as you open the fridge to get out eggs, bread and the jar of coffee. Things don't feel right, but when have things felt right in this strife-torn, divided land? You worry about the future. Your immediate future. The future of all who belong to this land. When the electricity comes on, you'll switch on the news and hear multiple, confusing accounts on multiple channels, explaining the why, what and how of Osama bin Laden's death. But what will all that news really reveal? What would Osama's death eventually mean for you, your beloved, for this town, this country or the world?

Suddenly, while whisking the eggs and vanilla and sugar, you surrender to the unanswerability of your questions; and yet all you can do to know you're alive is to keep asking the questions. She makes the coffee and you lower egg-soaked slices of bread onto the hot griddle. The knots of anxiety begin to dissolve as you turn your attention to the delicate, easy-to-break slices, slowly sizzling and firming, transforming from creamy yellowness to blotched caramel brown.

The two of you will sit down to breakfast soon. The immutable pull of something precious and elemental will draw you away from the forced, all-too-familiar world of unconquerable terror, of unresolvable doubts and fears, of unpredictable causes and their inevitable effects. At that moment, you'll be far from the world of deceitful news dished out on the news channels daily, like glitzy fast food. You will be grateful for no electricity and no TV and the silence, and the soothing aroma of freshly brewed coffee and vanilla from the caramelized French toast.

—⁂—

After breakfast, you will sit on the threshold between the dim, cool living room and the sun-lit balcony and scribble in your journal:

Rumi and Shams were lovers. Shams became Rumi and Rumi became Shams and both became a part of Eternal Reality. If the beloved is a shadow reflecting the lover, then Rumi was both Shams's shadow and God's. We are in seclusion like Rumi and Shams on the morning after Osama's death. Seclusion alone can bring us clarity. Seclusion alone offers us a chance to be ourselves.

I feel pregnant with a new love in this seclusion. I must protect it. I must disregard the world of manufactured good and evil, the Americans, the Taleban and the al-Qaeda. I'm staying on. Because it is now, it is here that I must nurture this pure love with all my devotion and attention, without giving in to distractions. Everything I've spent my life worrying about – safety, work, violence, wars, money, achievements, family – all were merely digressions, illusions.

There's harsh light outside and grey coolness inside the

living room and I'm sitting at the border of two worlds. Sheltered from the harshness of that hate-filled, veiled world and resting in the soft grey light of this indefinable love. How to nurture this sweet, nascent love if I return to that world of safety and yet inexplicable terror? She says that this is the very soil in which our love can grow. How long, how hard will we have to push to clear space for it to do so?

6

Sharmaji's Shoes

The day Sharmaji sent off the filled-up registration form for the annual retreat at the Krishnamurti Foundation was the day his wife said she was leaving. She didn't say she was leaving *him*. She said she was going to visit his daughter, Baby, in America. Baby was going to have a baby.

'When did you plan all this?' he asked her, surprised. 'How long are you going for?'

'I'm not sure…six months.'

He was outraged. 'Six months? Six months! What will you do for six months in America?'

'What do I do here?'

Her reply took him by surprise. She had never spoken to him in such a brazen manner and they had been married twenty-five years. When she spoke to him, it was always with a certain diffidence and respect, as if he were a priest or a schoolmaster. Their marriage was about roles and rules. *What do I do here*, he thought. What was she trying to tell him? That he made her work for him? He suddenly wanted to pin down her exact feelings in this matter, get clarifications, absolve himself of blame. What did the veiled hostility mean? Where had she acquired such nerve? When had she learnt to talk like this? But what if she really wasn't planning to return in six months? He gathered himself and went about his day, drinking his tea in sullen silence, watching the discourse on one of the spiritual channels, distractedly eating his breakfast and taking a very long time in the bathroom, shaving and bathing.

'Living and dying is the theme of this year's retreat,' he announced at lunch, to smooth over their morning ruffles.

But she went about her duties, bringing him fresh rotis from the kitchen. All she said was, 'You should tell the maid when you'll be returning. She'll cook for you.'

He was hurt by her matter-of-factness. 'The maid? You asked her to cook for me? She can't cook. What makes you think she can cook?'

'Then who'll cook for you when I'm not here?'

He changed the topic. 'I want to know why Baby didn't ask me to go and visit her. Or send a ticket for me. Am I not her father? Don't I want to see my grandchild?'

Baby was his daughter from his first wife, but whenever she called, she preferred to talk to her stepmother.

When she had cleared the table, Sharmaji's wife said, 'If you went with me, you would get bored.'

'Bored? What makes you think I would I get bored? I could go for walks, I could talk to Baby and her husband and their friends. Don't they have many weekend parties?' After a pause, he added, 'And I could play with the baby.'

She shook her head. 'No. You would get bored.'

He found her new self-confidence unnerving. How could she be so sure he would get bored? Mrs Sharma the Second, he had named her. She was much younger than him and he had only realized on their wedding night how young she was. Any other man in his position would have felt jubilant. But he was embarrassed by the years separating them and the gulf between them widened when they discovered they had very little to say to each other. She had become an ideal second wife, never opposing him, never going against his wishes. He was a widower with two children and in her, he found

the woman who would make a good mother. A man needs a
woman. And Mrs Sharma the Second needed a man and a
house. On the very next morning after their temple wedding,
she quietly assumed the duties of wife and mother as if she
had trained for it all her life. She didn't complain. She spoke
only when spoken to. Even in bed, she was soundless. He
never knew if she was experiencing pleasure, pain or nothing
at all. Intimacy between them had declined over the years
and she never indicated that she missed it.

The morning after she left for America, he tried to
overcome his feeling of dejection. He drank the maid's
watery tea without complaining. Some of it had spilled into
the saucer when she set it down with a thud. Sharmaji poured
the spilled tea back into the cup, hoping to make a point with
her, but she had already moved into the kitchen and was
chopping vegetables for his lunch.

He waited for almost a week to hear from Mrs Sharma
the Second. Finally, swallowing his pride, he called her.

'Hello?' he said when the phone was answered. 'All well in
America? Does anybody care to know how I am?'

Baby had answered the call, but handed the phone to
her stepmother. Instead of asking him how he was, his wife
enquired if the maid was working well.

'No, she's not. I don't like her cooking. You know she can't
cook. She can't even make a decent cup of tea. When are you
coming back?'

Mrs Sharma said she didn't know when she was coming
back.

Afterwards, he remembered he had forgotten to ask when
Baby's baby was due.

—∞—

As his relationship with Mrs Sharma the Second fell into
a predictable pattern, Sharmaji had focussed more on his

afterlife by giving up thinking about carnal pleasures. He started attending spiritual gatherings and never lost hope that Mrs Sharma the Second would also accompany him one day. Just before she told him she was leaving, he had stood at the entrance to the kitchen and read aloud from the leaflet:

'This gathering's focus will be on living and dying. Dying is a part of living,' he went on. 'So living, loving and dying are the same thing...do you hear? Did you hear what I just read out?'

He was a little unclear about how living, loving and dying were the same thing, but it had to be true if his spiritual guru said so. He wanted to explain it to his wife, to his doctor son in the UK, to his daughter in the US. But Mrs Sharma the Second wouldn't drop whatever she was doing in the kitchen and listen.

When his lawyer friend, Guptaji, called at night, Sharmaji persuaded him to join him for the retreat. 'Remember, what a good time we had last year?' he said.

That was where he had met Guptaji for the first time. He enjoyed his company and the food was great. They were served gulab jamuns every day. Sharmaji had continued to call Guptaji regularly. The last time he called, Guptaji casually mentioned that his wife had moved to her father's house. When? Why? For how long? But his friend didn't divulge any details.

So Sharmaji tried to make light of their shared plight. 'Wakeel sahib, we are both in the same boat now!' he told his friend. 'We have both become bachelors. My wife has gone to America. Yours has gone to her maika.'

—⁂—

The two men arrived at the retreat around the same time and Sharmaji greeted Guptaji warmly. But soon, things began to sour. Especially after Sharmaji's shoes went missing. He was hoping for compassionate sharing and unburdening and was hurt by Guptaji's barely veiled disdain when he went about scrutinizing other people's footwear. He could sense Guptaji sneering at him. Discussions on living and dying faded into fuzziness. Sharmaji couldn't concentrate any more. His attention was taken up by the loss of his new Nikes. How could somebody steal his shoes at a spiritual gathering? Baby had gifted him those Nikes on her last visit and he had kept them in their original carton, wrapped in tissue paper, to take out on a special occasion.

He had placed them just outside the entrance to the lecture hall. But an hour later, they were gone. He stared in disbelief at the spot where he had left them. He walked up and down the hallway, hoping somebody might have mistakenly placed them at another spot, pausing in despair at every pair of shoes and sandals to scrutinize them. He waited as people came out of the hall, slipped on their shoes and departed. In the end, there was only a worn out and ready-to-discard pair of red and white sneakers. Sharmaji slipped them on unwillingly, as if slipping into another life. They were a size too big and as soon as his toes came in contact with the sweaty, dusty insides, he cringed. His toes curled in protest. He limped across the lawn in the red and white shoes. His feet refused to relax in them. It was a strange, unclean feeling, accepting the clamminess of a pair of shoes belonging to another man. Maybe, somebody would bring back his shoes and leave them outside the lecture hall? His hope led him to make several visits to the hall that day.

Guptaji was attending a parallel session in another hall. He guffawed when he heard about the loss of Sharmaji's Nikes. This was worse than losing the shoes.

'Arre, Sharmaji, kya hua?' he asked. 'It's just a pair of shoes. Next time, you should do what I do. I separate the pair. I put one here and one there. Nobody steals just one shoe.'

'Guptaji, you're laughing? Do you realize we are in a sacred, spiritual place? We're not at a railway station. Who steals in such a place?'

The lawyer retorted, 'Spiritual place? What do you mean? Do you think people are different in a spiritual place, as compared to how they are at the railway station? People are people, Sharmaji. Same everywhere.'

'No, Guptaji,' Sharmaji countered. 'Not everybody is the same. How many people at a railway station would be interested in attending a spiritual gathering? Only a select few come to such places. Even my wife is not interested in attending.'

'Your wife is probably only too happy to be left alone. I think our wives enjoy things more without us. But you should tell her to come back from America after your grandchild is born.'

'Guptaji, why are you changing the topic? Why talk about my wife when I'm talking about my shoes? This is a philosophical question. Can there be thieves among spiritual seekers? If there are thieves among us, then what's the point of coming to a retreat like this? Somebody stole my shoes. If I tell my wife, she'll say she doesn't think much of people who come here.'

'Then you better not tell her! But how can you be so sure your shoes were stolen by a spiritual seeker? It could be one of the servants. They were Nikes, na? Bhaiya, the bugger will sell them and make more than his monthly salary.'

They had settled for the night in their cots which lined the dormitory walls like many others. The others had not yet returned from the after-dinner discourse. Sharmaji had yanked off the repulsive red and white stinkers and washed his feet to remove any clinging traces of sweat, dirt and stickiness, soaping and re-soaping his long, almond-shaped toenails. His first wife, his first love, had loved his toenails. She used to call them 'my eight almonds'. He dried his feet and slipped on his bathroom slippers. Mrs Sharma the Second had never evinced any interest in his toenails.

'All I have now are my bathroom slippers and those smelly shoes left by the thief!' he muttered in disgust.

Sharmaji rested his head on the pillow and looked up at the ceiling through the mosquito netting. The lawyer's cleverness was irritating. Sharmaji didn't want clarity or cleverness and clear-cut solutions. He wanted depth and compassion and debate on the deeper questions about right conduct. He didn't know how to express this. He stared at the peeling plaster on the ceiling, split up into a thousand fuzzy little squares through the netting, and said, 'Your good advice is a bit late, Guptaji.'

'Sharmaji, I'm a lawyer,' the other man told him. 'My advice is always timely. It's up to you what you take from this experience. I always learn from experience. How to put one foot here, one foot there. If you do that, you will never lose.'

It was Sharmaji's turn to puncture his friend's exasperating certitude. 'So Guptaji,' he said, 'when is *your* wife coming back?'

'She'll come back today if I tell her to, but I don't, because her father is – how should I put it – in the last stages of life.'

'My wife will also come back today if I ask her, but I don't,' Sharmaji countered. 'My daughter needs her.'

'That is no reason for your wife to stay on indefinitely. Life without the wife must be difficult for you?'

Guptaji was becoming more and more unkind and intrusive. So Sharmaji opened the Krishnamurti booklet he had received as part of the welcome package and proceeded to read:

'If somebody told you that you were going to die at the end of the day, what would you do? Would you not live richly for that day? We do not live the rich fullness of a day. We do not worship the day; we are always thinking of what we will be tomorrow…'

He read those lines several times, but the words didn't make any sense. How did one live richly and fully every day, with so much plaguing the mind? How to focus on the richness of each passing moment, when each moment was besieged by some unpleasant thought? How to remember that each day was made up of many noteworthy moments? He'd been reading Krishnamurti every day like he read the newspaper. But he still didn't know how to make sense of what he read or live according to the teachings, how to die every day, how to die before dying, how to free himself from the movement of thought and time. He had stopped going to the temple and given up the gods he grew up worshipping, but he still hadn't found the answers to questions: what would become of him after death? What lay beyond death? Why was death not really death? Would he have to come back to life? Or was this his last lifetime? Could he hope to meet Mrs Sharma, his first wife, when he arrived at the other shore?

At last year's gathering, he had bought seventeen Krishnamurti books and couriered them to his doctor son in the UK.

'Do you know what he did with those books?' He was addressing Guptaji now, though a few minutes ago, he had decided he wouldn't speak to him at all.

'What books?'

'Krishnaji's books. I had sent them to my son and he sent them all back to me. Arre, he could have donated them to a library! They have many libraries in the UK. And can you believe this, he wrote me a note: "Please don't send me such books again. It is a form of violence to force your views upon others."'

'Sharmaji, young people nowadays, especially if they live

abroad, have their own ideas about everything,' Guptaji told him. 'They don't want to be told what to think.'

'How can sending spiritual books by a man who has changed my life be a form of violence?'

Sharmaji willed himself to say no more to Guptaji. He wished he could talk to someone who would listen without shooting him down with readymade answers. He wanted to give vent to his feelings, his heartache, but the fear of receiving more clever rebuttals deterred him. He ached to speak of how hurt he was, because Mrs Sharma the Second hadn't called him even once. But how could he, when he was made to feel as if everything was somehow his own fault? He wanted tenderness and receptiveness of heart to speak of the differences between his first and second wives.

His own heart was burdened and he wanted to lay it bare. He wanted to pour out feelings he hadn't fully acknowledged even to himself. He wanted to share how his first wife's death had unmanned him; a man like him, an army man who had fought three wars for his country had not had an opportunity to get angry, to blame God, to weep off his grief. He had remarried, instead. He was sixty-five now and still in good health. Yet why did he feel it was best to rise above all worldly desires? This was puzzling. He wanted to renounce desire, but desire was keeping him chained. He couldn't confess that he woke up in the middle of the night with his heart thudding, longing to be held and soothed. Longing to be embraced. Who could embrace him? It was an infantile yearning for a safe corner, a tucked-away haven where his inner child could rest. Mrs Sharma the Second had never offered such womb-like shelter. She had moved out of their bed and into Baby's room after Baby got married. He lay awake most nights, alone, and imagined the different ways in which death could come. The thought of dying suddenly in this very bed and nobody finding out till the next morning scared him.

Guptaji was yawning and the other guests had started trickling in for the night. So Sharmaji returned to reading Krishnamurti, until the familiar words lulled him to sleep.

—∞—

Next morning, Sharmaji was at the receptionist's desk. 'Mistake?' he was saying. 'No, no, madam! No mistake-wistake. How can there be a mistake? The moment you step into somebody else's shoes, you know they are not yours. If it was a mistake, I would have got my shoes back by now. My shoes have been stolen.'

She noted down his complaint in her register, but her attention was diverted by other complainants.

'Madam, I'm telling you mosquitoes were biting all night,' said one. 'The mosquito net has holes. Please change the net or provide me an AllOut.'

'Madam, I have room with Indian toilet,' said another. 'I'm eighty years old. I made a special request for Western toilet. Can you give me room with commode?'

Sharmaji waited to ask the receptionist about his shoes. But he could see that she had more urgent problems to deal with. He left her and walked down the cobblestone path leading to the vast, sunlit lawn. Along the periphery of the lawn were the rooms for small group discussions that were held after every morning's lecture. He took off the sweaty red and white sneakers and decided to walk barefoot. Two peacocks darted away as soon as they saw him approaching. He paused to gaze at their iridescent plumage as they took flight. His mind couldn't register their beauty. Nor did the silver-speckled river beyond appeal to him much. Yellow butterflies flitted about and restless parrots screeched as Sharmaji passed under a tree. In previous years, all this had delighted him, but today, nothing did.

The facilitator opened the discussion by asking why, after

listening to so many of Krishnaji's talks and reading so many of his books, most people were still caught in the movement of their egos? He suggested that they had to reflect on this in total silence. Sharmaji's own mind was hardly ever silent or reflective. He was trying to gauge which one of the men in the room could possibly be the shoe thief.

—∽—

The following morning, Sharmaji hurried along the path accompanied by the 'hu-hu-hu' of the doves from the gnarled tamarind trees. He arrived at the reception before the other participants could do so, with their complaints, and put on a smile as he approached the desk.

'Madam, namaste,' he said. 'I am happy to see that you are not as busy today as you were yesterday. Have you had your breakfast?'

The woman nodded and looked up from her register. She had noticed his smile. 'Oh, it's you, Sharmaji. No news about your shoes?'

He seized the opportunity. 'No, madam, no news. But you're so kind. You remembered my name. I am honoured. You know, I am quite good at reading palms. Would you like me to read yours?'

'Achha! If you can tell me a few things quickly...' The woman put down her pen and offered him her right hand, palm facing up.

'I can tell a lot, madam. Give me both your hands. Spread out your palms like this.'

'Sharmaji, what do you see? Any money?'

'I can see a lot more than money. You are an extremely fortunate woman! You'll live to be a hundred years old.'

'What good is a long life without money?'

'No, no! It's going to be a good life in every way. Your life line is very strong and unbroken. But this! Madam, this is amazing! Just look at this diamond! Do you see it? This here, this diamond!' Sharmaji picked up the pen and traced a diamond in her right palm. 'A most rare thing! You don't find it in everybody's hand. Do you know what this diamond means, madam?'

The woman looked at him expectantly.

'This diamond is about something else!'

The receptionist stared at the blue ink diamond on her palm.

'This diamond means you've been gifted your final lifetime in this life. Liberated from the cycle of rebirth! Freedom from rebirth. True wealth, madam, the real thing. Congratulations, madam!'

The receptionist looked up at him. She seemed unconvinced. Liberation from rebirth was not a trivial thing, but she was hoping to hear something more beneficial.

'Thank you, sir,' she said. 'Life is hard, so it's just as well if I don't have to come back again. You've been coming here for many years, sir?'

'Do you know why I keep coming back? Because of good, honest people like yourself. I've gained much from meeting like-minded souls who are seeking answers to the same questions as I am. About life and death and what lies beyond. Only this time, I had bad luck. Instead of gaining, I have lost.'

The woman said she would, once again, make the announcement about his shoes. He heard the announcement over the loudspeakers. It was the last day of the gathering, his last day of hope.

―⁕―

That night, after dinner, he walked towards the river filled with rising resentment – he, a respectable, retired army man who had fought in three wars and won medals for bravery was reduced to tottering about in some stranger's old, filthy, oversize shoes. The moon had risen to the right of the temple. He sat on top of the ghat steps going down to the river, rubbed some Odomos on his arms and neck and studied the moon's image in the sluggish river. He couldn't say why the trembling reflection of the moon reminded him of his first wife. Even in his youth, he hadn't been prone to sentimental outpourings, but tonight, the shimmering moon reminded him of her. He stretched out against the thick trunk of an old neem. The moon's silver reminded him of her hair when she washed it and let it fall in waves down her back. His eyes watered as he looked at the flickering lights of vehicles on the faraway bridge. Cars seemed to be crawling like giant glowing ants. It was a cool night and the gnarled neem, the softly rippling river, the moon and the chanting from the temple unfurled desires he had long ago despatched to distant corners of his heart. He lay stricken by the weight of his longing. Memories rose and made him feel unsettled.

She was awaiting him in the bridal chamber, his bride, bundled up in gold and silk, the bed strewn with roses and jasmine – their first night of togetherness. He was at a loss for words. He put his arms around her and she turned to rest her head on his shoulder, as if she had been resting it there all her life.

He could feel her lips on his skin and his whole body opened up with an enormous yearning. To remember her by the light of the moon on the river was to taste her lips. He lost all sense of body; he was one with something much greater than himself. She was turning her head away playfully as he pulled her to himself. She was clasping him to herself in a gentle, almost motherly way.

He couldn't tell who she was or who he was. Their bodies were wrapped around each other. Then slowly, she began to untangle herself, setting him back on earth, setting desire ablaze with her fingers and lips, spreading out over him like a mythical, forest-growing creeper. Falling under her spell, he fell fast; he became limitless, rising above and beyond her, the river, above the moon, merging with the night sky.

He sighed with joy and exhaustion, 'You know how to treat a man like a king.'

'Bhaiya? Do you need help? Are you lost?'

'No, no, I'm not lost!' he said abruptly and stood up to face the man addressing him.

It was late. He trudged back, picking his steps carefully in the dark, wondering what had come over him by the river.

Back in the dormitory, he said to Guptaji, 'Did you see the moon?'

'No. Since when have you become a moongazer, Sharmaji?'

'I went for a walk and sat by the ghat. What a moon! Like a bride.'

'So you armywalas can also have feelings! Tell me, why was tonight's moon so special?'

'Tonight's moon…what can I say? Did I ever tell you about my first wife?'

'Your first wife? No.'

'The moon was like her. When I came back from the '71 war, she was already very ill; and in a month's time…' Sharmaji's voice trailed off. 'In a month's time, she left me. She died of cancer.'

He stared at his toes, unable to tell the other man how much she had loved his toes. What was breaking his heart? In what language could he speak of her koel-like voice, when she soaked his feet in warm water, scrubbed his soles with pumice stone, clipped his toenails – her beloved almonds – and dried his feet with her gentle hands. His feet would tingle just watching the movement of her head and hands. In what words could he speak of that long-forgotten rapture that leapt up from the soles of his feet and spread upwards and enveloped him?

He took out his handkerchief and wiped his eyes.

Guptaji watched him. 'Sharmaji...you never told me. I'm sorry. What to do? Death comes for all of us, sooner or later.'

Sharmaji spoke only after he had stashed away those unsteadying feelings somewhere deep and safe.

'Yes, Guptaji, my fate. The injustice of it. Why did she have to die so young? And leave me with two children? I had found happiness, but the gods didn't like it. I didn't really want to marry a second time. But what could I do?'

'Was she your first love?'

'First and only love! The only one who knew how to make me happy.'

Sitting by the ghat, he had revisited her, his home, their room, their bed, had caressed her girlish shoulders and her arms through her tight-sleeved blouse, had played with the pearls in her earlobes, stroked her long hair cascading down her back, had clasped her to himself, had pleaded with her not to torment his hunger with her touch and ended up murmuring, 'You know how to treat a man like a king.'

Being treated like a king by her was no ordinary stroke of luck. With her, he yearned to become a better man, simply because she believed he could. And twenty-five years of separation from her had only intensified that yearning. Who was he? Who was he really? Behind the retired army man that the world called Sharmaji, was there another man neither he nor the world knew? Thoughts of dying without ever coming to know this man were sprinkled with other thoughts about long-buried intimacies and the havoc played on skin with lips and fingers.

'Life is cruel, Guptaji,' Sharmaji said, careful in his use of words so as not to reveal his disturbing experiences by the ghat. 'But why, then, do I still want to go on living? Why are we afraid of death?'

He opened the K book on living and dying and read

aloud. The lawyer got up to turn off the light. 'Sharmaji, all I know is, life goes on. What is this life? Life is what we make of it. All this philosophical talk about living and dying is okay for these gatherings. You remember that song? *"Jeena yahan, marna yahan, iske sewa jaana kahan"*? Here is all there's to life.'

On the last day of the gathering, Sharmaji bid his friend good-bye. Their friendship seemed to have suffered and he wasn't sure he would meet Guptaji at next year's retreat. He bought a pair of cheap sandals from a roadside cart near the railway station and tossed out the red and white sneakers into a garbage heap.

—∽—

Back in Delhi, Sharmaji joined a laughter-therapy group. They were a group of men who laughed all the way to the neighbourhood park and back. Each one cracked a joke and then everybody laughed till the next joke. He knew very few jokes. After a few days of pretending to laugh at jokes that didn't really make him laugh, Sharmaji stopped going out with the laughter group.

He was watching the spiritual channel on TV. A young guru in a saffron lungi with a thick crop of hair and an equally thick covering of chest hair was addressing his audience with great confidence. 'Depression? What is depression?' the guru asked, then paused and smiled. He looked a little sinister to Sharmaji. 'When people come to me and say they are depressed, I laugh.' And the guru threw back his head and laughed. 'Do you know what I tell them? I tell them you are not depressed, you are just obsessed. Obsessed with yourself. All the time, thinking about yourself. "What will happen to me? What will my future be like?" You are depressed, because you are obsessed. No obsession, no depression. If they don't listen, I tell them to get lost. If I hug them and hold their hands and let them cry and cry, they'll never get over their depression.'

The bell rang. It was the maid. Sharmaji was parched for a few words with another human being. The maid placed a cardboard carton by the door and made her way to the kitchen.

'What's in the box?' he asked.

'I found it downstairs. The guard told me he was going to throw it out. I said, "Why do you want to throw it? It's a life. I'll take it home for my daughter." Her dog, Moti, died and she keeps crying.'

Sharmaji crouched by the carton and lifted the flap. Inside was a kitten, small and trembling. He reached in and lifted it, stroking its warm, fuzzy back. 'Why don't you see if it will drink some milk?' he called out. 'Also make me some masala chai. And have a cup yourself. Don't forget to add ginger.'

7

Aab-e-Hayaat

She leans against the parapet on the roof.

What if I end up dead like her? What if I fall and die for sure? But there's a chance I'll end up on some hospital bed, my mind sharp as nails, my body numb as a sponge.

She pulls back.

Boys on other rooftops are straining skywards, clutching spools of kite string and shouting. The desperate flutter of kites and boyish voices sink into her with the late-afternoon torpor as she makes her way down the stairs.

She has repeatedly imagined drifting into a quiet death, floating away without demanding too much care or attention, without lingering. A gentle death. Without violence. Not the kind of death her neighbour fell to. She remembers the wailing women bathing her neighbour's corpse. The woman had plummeted down; the loose bricks of the parapet had given way when she went up to collect the laundry. They used to chat on the landing in the hot evenings, while their children played downstairs. She would speak of her husband's absence and about his occasional weekend visits, which would turn her into a busy woman of the house. Flustered, brow furrowed, she would bury herself in her kitchen. She would stuff his tiffin box with his favourite dishes and he would carry the loaded tiffin box back on the train to the small town he worked in.

When he was gone, she would appear on the landing once more. 'He hardly speaks with me,' she would say wistfully, addressing her, but facing the still, unstirring air. 'And even less with the boys.'

The day she fell from the roof, neither her husband nor her sons were with her to ease her frenzied breathing before her body became still.

—∞—

On the flight to the city of her in-laws, she looks across the aisle at her husband and her daughter.

Do I know them? I'm supposed to know them intimately, but I'm not sure I do.

This unsettling thought leads to other frightening thoughts. *I don't belong to them. There's no relationship, no ownership without belonging. We are just balls of energy. How can you expect a ball of energy to own another ball of energy? How can one possess or be possessed by that which is substanceless? Formless? Undefined?*

At night, in her in-laws' flat, she can't sleep. She enters the dark living room and throws open the windows. The scene is set for a play just about to begin. Two men, with their backs to her, are sitting on the railway tracks across the street. What or who are they waiting for? Another man passes by on a bicycle. After he has gone, the street settles into its desolate look again. Except for the two men sitting on the tracks and her, watching them, there are no witnesses to this silent play in which she is both actor and spectator. The street has changed into its nightly garb; no longer the bustling, noisy thoroughfare it is during the day, it wears a smoky, haunted look. The eerie glow from streetlights hovers over the two men. The newly sprouted leaves on the Ashok trees gleam bronze-gold. An hour passes, maybe, two; she still sits watching them…

The latch on the gate clinks. The streetlights have gone out. A deep blue dawn is about to break. The latch on the gate clicks open. The newspaper delivery man has arrived. He is quick – in and out in an instant. She hears the latch click again as he leaves. Astride his motorbike, he's hurrying on to the next building. If only she could muster as much of a sense of purpose, if her life could be as packed with things to do from dawn to dusk so that she had no time to squander staring at strange men sitting on railway tracks. It is an affliction of the unoccupied.

—m—

She's back to what she's got into the habit of calling her house over the years, where she is even less sure of her relationship to her surroundings, whose vast emptiness seldom leaves her.

I suppose I'm depressed. I'm not supposed to be depressed. Life's not that bad. Things aren't that bad. Food. Shelter. Money. Don't I have it all?

'Life isn't that bad,' she repeats, but repetition doesn't lead to conviction. She repeats the list of affirmations she has copied from a self-help website to prop up her fast-fading sense of self. She comes out of the shower and standing in front of the mirror, repeats each affirmation ten times. *Life is good. I am good. Every day, in every way, I'm getting better and better.* But why, why should she repeat what doesn't feel true? Because that's how things begin to *feel* better eventually, say the self-help gurus. Fake it till you make it. Life's not a bed of roses for anybody. Every cup is either half-full or half-empty. The optimist tries to focus on the cup's fullness, the pessimist on its emptiness.

Well, I'm no optimist, I suppose.

But on some days, she is. She manages, after repeating the

list of affirmations, to see her cup as half-full. She thanks the
Sustainer for her privileges: house, husband, child, maid. But
on other days, when she's totally honest with herself, her cup
gapes at her, totally empty.

'I'm waiting for you to go to college, so I can leave this
prison,' she says to her daughter.

'But, Mamma, why do you call your home a prison?' the
girl retorts. 'So many women are living much worse lives.
What makes you feel imprisoned? I don't understand why
you can't be happy here. You are free to do whatever you like.
Write, read, travel. So why talk of leaving?'

She replies, shielding herself from the familiar accusation
of ingratitude, 'Free? Free? But I don't feel free! Have you
lived inside my head for twenty years?'

'What do you want to do? Where will you go?'

'I don't know. I'm tired of hearing how good my life
supposedly is.'

'You think you'll find freedom somewhere else? Away
from your family?'

How can she forget the family? How can she forget what
serving time in the family means? Who knows such security
better than her? How can she forget stability, protection,
sameness? Was it the fear of abandonment in her daughter's
heart that had made her ask, 'What's wrong with your life? I
don't understand why you can't be happy here.'

—⁂—

On a cool, blue morning in October, when she has expressly
asked the maid not to come before seven, she's the only one
to hear her ring the bell. She lies, corpse-like, hugging her
pillow, pretending, waiting fruitlessly for someone else to let
Binu in, even though she knows nobody will. The slow whir
of the fan above her almost drowns out the faint singing of
a bird outside. Beyond the window, beyond her husband's

white kurta-clad form, she glimpses the reckless swaying of the gangly, weak-trunked papaya tree. The room is bathed in blue light filtering in through the blue curtains they had bought together in the days when she was a good wife.

'What time is it?' asks her husband's sleep-muffled voice.

'It must be seven, because I told Binu to come at seven,' she replies irritably, sitting up, her feet feeling around for her slippers.

She unlocks the kitchen door, lets Binu in and returns to her side of the bed. But Binu wants to know what she is to cook for lunch, what she should do with the beans in the fridge. Will yesterday's bhindi be enough for today's lunch?

Will yesterday's bhindi be enough for today's lunch? Does she have to answer such questions so early in the morning? Can't anybody else answer them for her? Can't Binu make such decisions on her own after working for so many years in this house?

Her daughter sleeps through the morning, because there's no school due to a nationwide protest by Catholic schools over the killing and raping of nuns in Orissa. Just a moment longer, she thinks; if she could prolong this morning, stretch it out like a sheath that's not allowed to snap back, she could merge the blue shadows in the room with the floating thoughts in her head into an exquisite poem. She could stubbornly decide to stay in bed. But her daily anxieties are already on the march. Binu needs to be watched or she'll waste time in the kitchen, start flirting with the cleaner. The cleaner will be here soon. He has to be told he didn't do a proper job of mopping behind the toilet bowl. There are strands of hair lying on the floor. And the sink in the guest bathroom hasn't been scrubbed. She'll be the only one in the house to fret over hair on the bathroom floor and the unscrubbed sink.

She hears her husband in the shower. Why does he take these hurried showers? Why is he always hurrying to work?

'The water pump is on. Turn it off in an hour or so,' he instructs her, as he comes out of the bathroom.

'Okay,' she mutters.

It's not a death sentence, just instructions about the water pump, she muses, turning away from him to snuff out the rage that's foaming at her edges.

He senses her displeasure, the loss of her morning peace. Isn't he doing his share for the family? He's a good husband, a good provider. He can't help it if she doesn't want to see the maid or the cleaner in the morning or check on the water pump.

'I'm worried, because there wasn't enough water in the tank upstairs,' he explains, continuing to violate her morning solitude.

Water! Water is an urgent matter. Where would we be without water? She tries to disregard the infringement of space, imagines the room's walls caving in on her, sees herself wafting out, leaving behind her body, hugging the papaya tree. But her body falls back limply against the bed and her heart files away the theft of yet another morning in its secret ledger.

It's not his fault. But whose fault is it?

He continues, 'There was no power yesterday, so the pump didn't run. But now there'll be enough water if the pump runs today.'

Of course, there will be enough water if the pump runs today, if the power doesn't go off! If she does what is expected of her, there'll be enough water for everybody in the house. She recalls the Phil Collins song, 'It's another day in paradise,'playing in the cyber café of that mountain retreat she had managed to escape to for a week last year.

Self-deprecation is a hard-to-kill habit and like a daily dose, she swallows its poison. Her repetition of affirmations today is not effective as an antidote to the poison of self-hatred coursing through her veins:

You're a privileged woman. You're a fortunate woman. You know the struggles of other women? You know what time Binu has to wake up to be at your house at six or seven? And you mourn the loss of a mere morning?

There are no silent mornings for Binu.

But does Binu want silent mornings?

Do you know what the life of those nuns in Orissa was like, the ones who ran the orphanage? The ones who got raped and killed?

No.

If only you could be more grateful for all you have.

Yes, if only I could be more grateful.

Fake it till you make it.

I've tried. You must believe me. I've tried for twenty years.

—⁓—

She's lying on the cool marble of the living-room floor. There's a fleeting stillness to the greying afternoon, with Binu finally gone and her daughter out. She's entreating God:

I feel alone, though I know you're with me. Why?

The answer, she senses, is wordless and voiceless and comes from somewhere within and beyond her − *you are not alone; you are your own teacher.*

I? My own teacher? I'm just a bitter woman, full of self-pity. Weak-willed. My sorrows are burrowing into my soul. I keep praying for a quiet death, because I can't manage a damn thing. How can I be a teacher to myself? I want to surrender at the feet of some greater being and her nazr-e-karam must save me. She hears the key turn in the front door. Her daughter has returned from her friend's place.

'Are you okay, Mamma?' she asks. 'Why are you lying on the floor? Can I sit with you? I want to talk to you. I just thought of something I wanted to tell you and you alone. Can I do "kuchu-kuchu" in your hair?'

'What do you want to tell me?'

'I want to tell you how a true friendship is like a crescent moon,' her daughter begins, running her fingers through her hair in slow circles.

She begins to feel drowsy from the 'kuchu-kuchu' as her daughter's fingers trace and soothe the pounding headache just under her scalp.

'How is a true friendship like a crescent moon?' she asks dreamily.

'Well, there's only a sliver of the crescent that's visible and rest of the moon lies hidden. What the world can see is just that crescent. What we truly feel lies hidden like the unseen moon. We can only sense it in our hearts.'

'And you think your friendship with your new friend is a crescent-moon friendship?'

Her daughter bends down to kiss her forehead.

Her phone rings and she leaves the room. It's probably the crescent-moon friend calling. She drifts deeper into her dreaminess. A friend in the States had emailed her a link to an online meditation site. Midas Jump was about raising your self-esteem by meeting your ideal twin self. She was about to delete the link, since the long-haired man giving the instructions looked like one of those New Age gurus she was tired of watching on YouTube. But for some reason, she decided to give him a hearing.

She closes her eyes now and remembers his words: 'Imagine yourself as you would like your ideal self to be. What would you have been like if you had a different upbringing? If you made different choices in life?'

Right! Let's imagine: what would I have been like if I had made different choices? If I'd had a different upbringing?

She sees a confident, creative, articulate woman sitting in a wide open, fresh-scented garden, surrounded by healing light. Her aura is brighter than all the other lights around her. She's smiling reassuringly as she approaches the bruised, battered woman who has just entered her enchanting garden. 'Where have you been?' she asks. 'You certainly took a very long time coming. But now that you are here, put up your feet and relax. Surrender all your anxieties. You don't need to go back to that other life, that prison of fears and self-doubt. We don't judge people here based on how they lived their lives. You can live here as long as you like. Or if you do have to leave, you can come back whenever you wish. Choose a quiet spot in the garden where you want to live and call it your own. The water here is sweet and cool and fresh from the springs. We call it aab-e-hayaat, the Water of Life, and it flows all year round. So drink without fear. And there's all the fruit you want to eat. And there's wine you love. You can get a massage too. I know your back hurts. There's a hot, fragrant tub waiting for you to soak in. Pick as many blossoms as you like from this garden and add them to the water for your bath. The birds are waiting to sing for you. And there's a library full of books. You can read, you can write, you can daydream. There will be no interruptions. I promise. Your mornings will be just the way you want them. There's lots of music too. There's a loft you can sleep in. And you can see the crescent moon rising from your window.'

She trudges up to this twin self, a figure of towering grace and healing gentleness, and bows, resting her head at her feet. Tears of exhaustion pour out. But she is encircled by a pair of strong, caring arms. She is raised to meet the mesmerizing gaze of her twin self. She lets herself collapse in those embracing arms. She thinks of crescent-moon friendships as she rests her head on the shoulders of this strong, gentle woman. Her crescent moon has risen on the night of her union with herself, on the night of celebration of the most primordial of marriages – of the self with the self.

8

Sunday Morning

The houses in the lane are asleep, lulled by the final days of fasting and feasting and last night's rain. It's the end of Ramzan and the householders are lying under heavy quilts after sehri and fajr prayers. Shabnam and her little sister had stirred when their parents got up for sehri, but had gone back to sleep. Now the girls awaken, cold and hungry in the still dark morning. They lie next to each other, their scant, warm bodies shivering under their quilt. They know there will be no rotis left for them. Shabnam knows there'll be no food until much later, until her Baba, who goes out to look for work every day, returns with something her mother can cook for iftar. If he finds work today. A whole day's guesswork stretches between now and iftar.

Shabnam nudges her little sister and together, they creep out of the room. They squint at the tandoor in the light of the just-breaking day, the tandoor that lies cold after it was lit to bake last night's bread. Their uncles and their wives and children are asleep in the other two rooms. The girls rub their hands up and down their bare arms to keep off the chill and slide their feet into their slippers. There's no water in the bucket, so they can't wash. Shabnam picks up the plastic jar with the eggs her hens have laid on the roof. Unwashed, the sisters make their way down the lane towards the large houses lining it. Two scrawny, scruffy girls.

It's very quiet, the tranquil quiet of a Sunday morning when people don't have to go to work or school. Shabnam thinks of cosiness and warmth, of curling up under a thick quilt. She thinks of the heavy quilts laid out on the large beds in the big houses, beds of children who don't have to get up and go out looking for food. On the way to the Baji's house, she sees a man trying to start his car and scurries past him. Will he stare, will he scold, will he curse at her and her sister? A rooster crows from the garbage dump. A curled-up street dog growls. A child coughs, then starts to whimper. The swish of a servant's broom from one of the houses blends with the clanging of a bucket.

Suddenly, two boys on bicycles whoosh past them, laughing and teasing.

Rascals! Shabnam curses them silently. *If they come again, I'll pick up a stone and smash their faces in.*

She makes and unmakes a fist with her free hand as the boys go snickering past. She yanks at her little sister's arm. The boys had just missed ramming their bicycles into her and nearly toppled her jar of eggs.

'Salaam, Baji,' Shabnam says in greeting to a woman who hurriedly walks past her. Two little girls are following the woman. In a whiny voice that Shabnam can never think of using with her own mother, they are begging her for something they want for Eid. The girls and the woman live in one of the houses in the lane. The woman keeps walking ahead, not paying heed to her whining daughters.

Shabnam and her sister reach the closed gate of the white house. Shabnam knocks and calls out. 'Baji! Baji, gand hai?'

There's no answer. She knocks again. The large white house remains mute.

She bangs her palm against its high green gate and calls out urgently, 'Baji! Baji! Gand hai?'

Shabnam and her sister flop down in the middle of the

lane. The shy winter sun is casting its slanting rays on the cold ground. The girls gather pebbles and stones and start playing, prepared to wait.

Two hens cluck around fussily, sifting the dirt and scratching the ground. Shabnam flings little pebbles at them to scare them away. Her sister grins and says, 'Hoosh! Hoosh!'

Shabnam can feel her empty stomach twist and heave. She hugs the jar and gazes fondly at the pale, tea-coloured eggs inside. Then agitated, she walks over to the gate of the large, white house.

'Baji! Baji! Gand hai?' she shouts in her hunger-sharpened voice and reaches up for the doorbell.

Finally, a young woman, a few years older than Shabnam, emerges from the house. Untidy wisps of her uncombed hair peep out from under the dupatta framing her pretty, sleep-rumpled face.

'Don't you know you shouldn't ring the bell so early?' she says irritably. 'It's Sunday. And it's Ramzan! People are trying to sleep, you know.'

'We were waiting a long time, Baji,' Shabnam says meekly. 'Do you need eggs? My hens laid them yesterday. And we can take out your gand.'

The pretty woman disappears into the house. She returns, carrying two plastic dustbins. One is large and green and laden with vegetable and fruit peel. The other is stuffed with paper and plastic wrappings.

'I'll take three of those eggs. Mother will pay you later. She's asleep now.'

'No, please! Take all six,' Shabnam pleads. 'They're fresh. You can pay me later.' She thrusts the jar with the fresh, frail eggs into the woman's hands.

Shabnam carries out the heavier dustbin and gives the lighter one to her sister. The thought of food is making them both skittish. They scamper down the lane to the garbage dump at the corner where they had seen the rooster. Her sister tries to keep up with her, but her feet keep slipping out of her too-small slippers. Shabnam empties out her dustbin and doesn't mind the stench that assails her nostrils. Two goats are searching through the garbage for scraps to eat.

Shabnam calls out to them playfully, 'Here, here, Bhai jaan, your breakfast is here!' and darts back to the house with the emptied dustbin.

The Baji opens the gate just a crack and wrinkles up her nose. 'They have to be rinsed,' she says, indicating the dustbins.

'Give us some water, then,' Shabnam says, disappointed.

'Get it from the bucket!'

Shabnam enters the courtyard and walks to the toilet in the corner. The water in the bucket is freezing and stings her hands, turning them red.

'Take the buckets outside,' Baji orders, her voice crackling. 'Don't pour the dirty water out into the toilet drain like you did the last time.'

Shabnam and her sister carry out the bins and pour the murky water into the open drain running alongside the lane. The Baji takes the bins back from them and disappears into the house.

Shabnam waits vacantly. She swallows her saliva to moisten the dryness in her mouth.

Baji returns with two rotis and a few pakoras, leftovers from yesterday's iftar, and hands Shabnam the empty egg jar.

Shabnam dries her raw hands on her kameez and receives the food. The gate shuts on them and the two girls are left standing in the narrow lane.

'Do you want the pakoras or one of the rotis?' Shabnam asks her little sister, tucking the empty egg jar under her arm and staring contemplatively at the rotis and pakoras.

'Both.'

'No! You can't have both. You have to choose!'

'You keep the rotis. Give me the pakoras,' her sister says greedily.

Shabnam had wanted the pakoras, but doesn't know why she slides them into her sister's outstretched hand. Her fingers close over the dry roughness of the rotis and she imagines dipping them in a glass of hot, sweet tea.

One pakora falls out of her sister's hand and into the dirt. The little girl bends down to swoop it up and wiping it on her kameez, pops it into her mouth and swallows it.

Shabnam scolds her. 'You can't eat in the street! It's Ramzan. They'll say bad things about us. Couldn't you wait?'

Shabnam isn't sure how old she is, if she's ten or twelve, but she is aware of the sort of things people say about them. Earlier, the people of this town used to call them 'those Afghanis' and they still call them that. She knows it's not proper to eat in the street during Ramzan. Even if you're very hungry and thinking about nothing but food.

Whenever she tries to ask how old she is, her mother lift her hands impatiently from the dough she's kneading, waves them about dismissively and says, 'Maybe, you're ten. Or maybe, twelve. Allah knows.' All Shabnam knows about her birth is that she was born in a tent. Just like her little sister and twin brothers. She had watched her mother writhe and moan when her siblings were born. She had kept peeping in from the gaps in the tent's flap. They lived in a camp near Peshawar then. She knew she shouldn't have watched, but all she did see was the midwife's broad, bent-over back.

'Allah has sent you two brothers,' her mother had whispered to Shabnam, her voice a soft moan, when she went into the tent later. Her mother had pointed to the two new red faces, swaddled in rags, and said, 'Allah is most kind.' That was the only time she heard her mother speak in such a feeble voice.

The surreptitious peeping in had made Shabnam much wiser, quieter and fiercer than her mother. After the boys were born, whenever she went up to the roof of the house to collect eggs from her hens, she never asked her mother to fry them for her. She would go out and not return home until she had sold every single egg and given her mother the money she had earned. She puzzled over the frequent lack of food in their home; she stared at the tandoor that remained unlit on days Baba didn't find work. On days when he didn't bring flour and vegetables and the tandoor stayed cold, she wanted to run away to some faraway place. She imagined living in a house with plenty of food. Why were they always hungry? Mother said Shaitan was responsible for their hunger. But who was this Shaitan? What did he look like? Shabnam wanted to believe her mother because her mother didn't tell lies. She had started seeing this Shaitan after her mother told her about him. He was the one sitting atop their cold tandoor. When she woke up and went out to the toilet by herself, when it was still dark, she had seen his evil eyes, glinting in the dark. One day when she didn't feel quite so frightened of Shaitan, she intended to walk up to him and ask him why he was doing this to her family.

9

Goodies

Until she met him at the airport, they had talked only on the phone. And on the phone, he had sounded quite sophisticated and suave, with his Oxford-Cambridge English. He was respectful, never tried to talk over her, never attempted to mansplain. He seemed to respect and appreciate her as a working woman. Which was a lot more than she could say about her last two husbands. A few weeks into their phone dates, he asked her if she'd like to get married and she said yes. He was much older, but a twice-divorced woman couldn't complain if a once-divorced, well-placed man of seventy proposed to her.

When she saw him appear through the exit, however, she had to pay attention to that uncomfortable feeling that was gnawing at her insides. Something about the way he walked – slowly, as if hanging on for support to the luggage trolley, his butt sticking out at an odd angle – alerted her. He looked confident, but much older than in the photos he had sent of himself on WhatsApp. *Mustn't judge in a hurry, mustn't feel disappointed* – she kept repeating the soothing mantra. She walked up to him and put on a cheerful, welcoming smile.

Considering he was seventy, his skin wasn't hanging loose on him, she noticed, and the Dubai sun had given it a honeyed tan. She was surveying him and knew he was surveying her too. It felt like they were customers checking out stuff at a store and this made her feel anxious. Where was this relationship, if she could call it a relationship, headed?

In the car, he took out a small box and slipped a shiny diamond ring on her ring finger.

'It's gorgeous!' she said. 'You shouldn't have.'

'I was afraid you might change your mind, darling, so I didn't want to take any chances!' he whispered, so the driver wouldn't hear him and lifting her ringed hand, kissed it.

His lips felt scratchy-papery on her skin and she pulled back her hand. She asked him to give the driver the hotel's name.

As the porter was loading his three suitcases onto the hotel's luggage trolley, he checked the man and said, 'No, no, not that one.' Then turning to her, he explained, 'That one's for you, darling.'

She felt flustered. 'For me? No, really?'

—∞—

After work, she had the driver bring up the suitcase to her apartment. She opened it in the privacy of her bedroom. Guccis, Bulgaris, Chanels and a Dolce & Gabbana handbag – all neatly wrapped in tissue paper. She felt unnerved by the scale of his gift-giving, but the thing that made her smile was the *Professional Pastry Chef* cookbook. He had remembered she wanted it and had ordered it for her!

She called up her daughter. 'Come over,' she said. 'Come and see all this fancy stuff he's got for me.'

Her daughter came over and inspected the handbags, the perfumes, the watches. 'Mamma,' she said, 'I have a feeling this stuff isn't real.'

'What do you mean it isn't real?'

'I think he picked it all up from some outlet mall in Dubai. They sell fake brands at those malls.'

'How do you know?'

'Come on, Mamma! It's obvious. Okay. Here, look at the spelling of Dolce & Gabbana.'

She looked closely. Her daughter pointed out the 'C' where there should've been a 'G' on the label on the buckle.

She laughed it off in her daughter's presence. But afterwards, it took a lot of effort on her part to not feel humiliated by the revelation that the man she was planning to marry had gifted her a suitcase full of fake goodies.

When he called, she hadn't yet recovered her composure.

'We're meeting for dinner, remember, darling?' he reminded her. 'An important friend and his wife will join us. I want you to look your very best.'

'I'm tired. I can't be bothered to dress up,' she told him.

'But darling, you must! I want to show you off. You must look absolutely stunning and gorgeous. Put on some of the things I got for you. And remember the high heels. Haven't you opened the suitcase yet?'

The dread she had felt at the airport deepened. Still, like one drowning, yet hoping to be rescued, she walked into the shower, picked out a black and silver-embroidered chiffon sari from her closet and matched it with the fake Dolce & Gabbana handbag with its misspelt label. She used her own perfume, not one of his, because fake stuff gave her skin rash. She put on make-up carefully. The painstakingly applied concealer, eyeliner and lipstick took a decade off her. She even remembered the high heels. As she slipped on his diamond ring, she made a note of having it evaluated by a jeweller she trusted.

At dinner, he introduced her to the others as a 'close friend'. This brought on a fresh wave of that heavy feeling, but she sat demurely, nursing her gin and tonic, determined to sink the whole evening into gin-induced oblivion.

He leaned over and whispered to her.

'Excuse me?' She hadn't caught the words.

'Your posture. Darling, your posture! You're slouching.'

She swam up from the abyss she had sunk into and pressed her back against the hardback chair, but soon drifted into inattentiveness.

During the evening, she stole several lazy glances at him, at his cigar-smoking friend and his overly made-up wife and wondered what it would take to lighten her heaviness. Nothing she saw matched what she had conjured up of him during those long, late-night phone conversations. What was even more frightening now was that the mismatch between image and reality was making her question her own susceptibility to getting fooled. *I'm fifty-five, for God's sake, and no wiser*, she told herself.

His upturned lips, dyed hair and moustache, his overbearing self-assuredness... She began to recoil from him. He suddenly reminded her of her first and second husbands.

Her phone rang. Her catering manager wanted instructions for the next day's big order. He called several times after that. She went out to the balcony to take the calls. Every time she returned, she could tell her host was displeased.

After his dinner guests had left, she too wanted to leave.

'Your phone rang too many times during dinner, darling,' he reminded her.

'It was my manager. I run a business, you know.'

'And another thing darling...your posture. It's most unfeminine to slouch that way. When we're in company, watch my left eyebrow. If I lift it twice, it means you need to sit up straight.'

She formed her own silent reply to that and hurled it at him.

'Let's have coffee,' he suggested.

'It's late. I'd better go home.'

'But we are meeting tomorrow for lunch, aren't we?'

'I'm not sure. I have a big order to deliver tomorrow.'

'Your manager can handle that, darling. I'll see you tomorrow at lunch.'

No, you won't!

Suddenly, this other woman inside her started screaming.

On her way to the car, one of the straps on the Dolce and Gabbana handbag came off. She looked down at it and wished it hadn't. But in a way, she welcomed the finality delivered by a sequence of fateful events. Her whole life had been a series of bad decisions. It swam before her now in the short time it took her to reach the car and collapse on the backseat.

All night, that woman inside her kept screaming at her, the one she hadn't paid much attention to in her two previous marriages.

Give me one reason why he should gift you fake brands! Give me one good reason why you should have to look stunning for his friends! Why you should have to wear high heels and sit up straight? Give me one good reason why he didn't introduce you as his fiancée!

Near dawn, the woman within her finally shut up and allowed her to fall into an uneasy sleep.

There were twelve missed calls from him when she woke up. She called back.

'Aren't you coming over for lunch, darling?' he asked.

'I can't.'

'I've come all the way from Dubai to be with you! We have a lot to plan, you know.'

'I told you I had a big delivery today. I'm late already. I have to be at work. And there's something else…er, I can't accept your gifts.'

'What do you mean you can't?'

'I can't. And I can't marry you.'

'For God's sake!' he spluttered. 'It was just last week that you agreed to marry me, to have a simple nikah. And what about our honeymoon in Thailand? You said yes to everything. You can't change your mind so suddenly.'

'I *am* changing my mind suddenly.'

The woman inside her finally breathed easy and the sense of foreboding that had hung over her began to subside.

'Don't you think you're being really childish, darling?'

'Oh, no! I think I'm being very wise. Please stop calling me "darling. You couldn't even introduce me last night as your fiancée! You see…er…there's this woman. She wants to know why…she… Well…well, let's just call her my wiser self. She's trying to save me. If I don't listen to her now… I mean…I have to or she'll kill me.'

'Who'll kill you? Who's this woman?'

She ended the call – no sweet good-byes, no explanations – and put her phone on 'silent'. Then she removed his ring from her finger. No need to get it evaluated. She placed the ring in its velvet box. She stuffed into the suitcase the Guccis, the Chanels and the Bulgaris, the ring and the Dolce & Gabbana bag with the broken strap, placing the bag above everything else, so he would see it first thing, and called the driver to come up and take the suitcase away, with express instructions to deliver it to the gentleman in his hotel room.

She returned everything – except the *Professional Pastry Chef* cookbook, which she took with her to bed to read and make a note of variations of pie-crust recipes for improving her own bakery's pie crusts.

10

The Rapist's Wife

She's changing the baby when the news comes on. A call-centre worker returning home from a friend's house has been raped by three men. One of the rapists is Satyadev, a married man with a child and owner of the mobile-phone shop the nineteen-year-old call-centre employee had often visited.

Satyadev! Is that *her* Satyadev? He too has a mobile-phone shop. And he didn't come home. His phone's been switched off since last night. She gives the baby his milk and sits down at the edge of the bed. She feels nothing, except a vast emptiness, as she stares distractedly at the running ticker tape displaying stock-market figures at the bottom of the TV screen. A shrill reporter's voice accompanies the rapidly moving images.

—∞—

Some months later.
Knock! Knock!
Who's there?
Your rapist's wife.
Silence. She knocks again. The door opens a crack.
Who are you?
I'm your rapist's wife.
What do you mean?

What I just said: I am your rapist's wife.

What do you want?

I've come to ask you something very important.

What?

Open the door a little. I can't talk standing outside. Let me in.

The door opens a little.

You heard the news, right? Your rapist has been sent to jail. I am his wife. I want you to come and live with me.

Why?

Because you and I, we need each other. We could keep each other company. We would be much safer and stronger living together.

This is crazy. I'm okay here by myself.

No, you're not! Have you looked at yourself in the mirror? Do you know how haggard you look! Anybody can see you're sad and lonely. And you hate yourself for what was done to you. I hate it too. We need each other.

Whoever heard of a rape victim moving in with her rapist's wife?

It's the most sensible thing. We've both been wronged. As soon as you see we're both his victims, you'll see what I mean. There's no problem in our living together. On the practical side, we won't have to pay two rents. You can keep your call-centre job. We'll share the housework. You can pay half the rent on my flat. My son will love you. I don't have much time to play with him. You could do that when you get off work. What do you say?

It's bizarre! This is just a story we're stuck in, right? Maybe, the writer of this story, she's manipulating us into saying what she wants to say?

I wouldn't worry about her. It's really about you and me. You have to understand. Stop thinking of yourself as a victim. You are a rape survivor. Just like me.

Have you been raped too? By whom?

The same man who raped you.

Really? What difference does it make if I call myself a victim or a survivor? I still have nightmares. I'm still taking sleeping pills and I still wake up sweating and crying in the night.

So do I.

What do you mean?

I told you I'm also his victim. I've had many sleepless nights too. But now I think of myself as a survivor.

You were his wife...so?

She nods.

I'm sorry, I never thought...I always thought...

I'm his wife, so it's okay for him to rape me?

I mean...no. It's not okay.

I could do nothing. I couldn't even scream and ask for justice. Which police station would file a wife's FIR against her husband for raping her?

I know this isn't about keeping count, but you were raped by one man. I was raped by several –your husband and his friends.

It's unforgivable.

'But why didn't you... Surely, you could've done something to stop him?

Like what? How do you ask your husband to stop? How do you know I didn't try? He would shut me up by saying it was my duty to let him have his way. He would hit me. I didn't mind him hitting me, but you know what made me give in?

What?

Fear.

Fear? Maybe, he wouldn't have had the nerve to do it if you had stopped him. He must have done this to other women too.

Fear of all sorts. Not just the fear of being beaten. He

would get drunk. He would come home and put on one of those films. Then he would call me. If I resisted, he would hit me and force me to watch the films. Those women in the films looked so sad, like me. They looked like clowns, all made up and pretending to enjoy themselves. I didn't ever feel a thing. But I pretended. All the time he would be doing his thing, I would close my eyes and pray. When it was over, I would thank God. I would feel sorry for the women in the films. They have to do it with hundreds of men on camera.

At least, they get paid for it.

Yes, I got paid too. That's why I was afraid he would leave me and I would have nowhere to go. I was always afraid he'd throw me out of the house. My mother didn't want me back. She said, 'Isn't he paying the rent and taking care of you and your son? What more do you want?'

I'm sorry. Why don't you sit down? Let me get you a glass of water. Or would you like tea?

Come with me. We'll make tea in my flat. I'll make you pakoras. I have a good feeling about this.

About what?

About us being together...don't you see? Everything had to happen the way it did...so we could come together. Become good friends and *saathin*. Be my *saathin*.

Wah! You're really optimistic. I haven't even told my parents about what happened to me. I don't have the courage.

You don't have to tell them. When he was sent to jail, I cried and cried and wanted to run to my mother's house and tell her what had happened. I cursed my fate. But I didn't. I knew what she would say. I was afraid she would just shrug and say all this happens. How many times had I thought of leaving him! But I couldn't. I had my son. I worried about his future. And then this thing happened and it was all over the news and I felt totally alone. And free in some strange way. I had nobody to turn to. I felt there was something new waiting for me in this madness. A voice spoke to me.

Whose voice?

God's voice. God wanted to bring us together as saathins. God wanted us to walk out of this nightmare together. I felt like a voice was urging me to come and find you. But it took some courage to find you. So now I've come after all these months.

What else did God say?

God said, 'Wake up. You've been stuck in a bad dream too long. Just because you've been stuck in it for years doesn't mean you can't ever get out. I command you to go to her. Her pain is no different from yours. Share your pain with her. You two can heal each other; together, you can build a different life.'

And so you came looking for me?

Not immediately. I tried to ignore the voice, but it was persistent. It became a nuisance. It didn't let me sleep or eat in peace. I thought I would go mad.

How did you find me?

I asked around. I had seen you at his mobile shop, but I didn't know then that it was you. We live upstairs in the same building. I knew I would find you, somehow. There's something mysterious about it all. I don't quite understand it myself. Do you believe in God?

Not anymore. Acha, if I move in with you and he gets out of jail and comes straight back home –then what?

Who says he has a home to come back to?

You're still married to him. Aren't you afraid of what he could do when he gets out?

I'm not stuck in that old dream anymore. So come with me. Don't say no. Let's build another life. Help me raise my son. We'll raise him to become a different kind of man. Don't you think that's worth doing? Think before you say no.

How can you be sure we won't be stepping into another nightmare worse than the one we're walking out of?

We have to step out of this one first, before we find out what the new dream will be like.

I'm confused. I'm scared.

I'm also confused. I'm scared. But I'm willing to take a risk.

You want to take a risk with me?

With you. Absolutely. Our pain unites us. You and I are saathins.

I wanted to die ever since this thing happened...

Nonsense! Why should you die? I used to think the same way. This dying-shying is going to get us nowhere. Have you ever thought why *we* should have to kill ourselves? We haven't committed a crime. Look, if you trust me, step out. If you don't trust me, don't step out – and we lose this chance of a lifetime.

Ever since that night, I've been wanting life to end.

No! No! Wish for life to begin! No more talk of dying. Together, we will be like the neem and the peepal tree. We will lean against each other.

Are you sure?

Yes. You don't trust me, do you? But if only you could...

If only I could.

You haven't had a good meal in a long time. What do you eat? You look so thin. Your hair looks like a broom. I'll massage it with hot oil tonight. Hurry! Get your things. I can't be here forever. I left my son with the neighbour and he'll start crying if I'm gone too long.

I still think this isn't going to work. What will my family say if they find out I've moved in with you – my rapist's wife?

But you haven't told your family about the rape.

That's true. I haven't. And maybe, I don't need to. They'll worry about me and they'll come and take me back to the village. I think all this worrying has taken away my ability to think....'

'Stop worrying. It's the story, our story that's important. We have to start living our story. Do you want to live the new story with me?

11

Arzi

'Are you writing an arzi?'

'Arzi?'

'You were writing something.'

'No, no…just some notes.'

'Can you write an arzi for me?'

'Arzi? I could try. I've never written one.'

'I'll tell you what to write. Write the number, seven hundred and eighty-six, on top and today's date.'

'And then?'

'Wait! I'm telling you. Write:

'*O Chandan Baba, salaam.*

'*I am Saroj. I'm a poor, unfortunate woman. I've come to you to tell you of my woes. Please listen to me and help me. I can't walk well because of the pain in my left leg. My daughter's wedding has been fixed for 10th June. Tell me, how am I to pay for her wedding? And my younger one, she is not normal. Bless her with peace of heart and mind. I have a little shop in the village, but it's not doing very well. Shower your blessings upon my shop and solve all my problems. I have nobody to turn to. Now I've told you everything.'*

'Is that all?'

'Yes, that's all. Tear out the page. Let me sign my name.'

'I thought you couldn't write?'

'I can't write an arzi. But I can sign my name. I'm going

to hang it on that string. See that wall? That's where. When Baba grants my wishes, I'll bring a new chadar for his tomb. Here, Ali, here's twenty rupees. Run off and get elaichi dana and one packet of agarbatti. Bring back the change. Hurry now.'

'What are you sprinkling on the arzi?'

'Attar my neighbour gave me. Smell it. It's chandan. I want to present a chandan attar to Chandan Baba.'

I took a whiff from the tiny vial. It was too strong and bore little resemblance to sandalwood.

'Who's Ali?'

'My neighbour's grandson. She sent him along, so I won't get lost. It takes many hours to get here. I'm just doing everything the way she told me to. We got on the bus at five in the morning.'

'Do you know anything about Chandan Baba?'

'I only know what she told me.'

'She?'

'My neighbour. My friend. Baba's real name was Chandan Singh. When he became a Musalmaan, they started calling him Chandan Shahid. He was a martyr in a war hundreds of years ago. His body lies here, but his head lies in that faraway place where he fell. His horse carried his headless body all the way to this very spot. The people of this village buried him here. When they touched his grave, the dust on their hands turned to chandan. Oh, Ali…did you get the elaichi dana and the agarbatti?'

'Where are you going now?'

'I told you, I'm going to hang the arzi. Then I'll give the elaichi dana to that man, that one, see? Next to the tomb. Then I will light the agarbatti and sweep the floor.'

Saroj proceeded to hang her arzi and I went and sat near the entrance from where I could watch all that was happening near the tomb. Men and women kept entering the shrine's inner sanctum to pray or plead at Chandan Baba's tomb, depositing their footwear at the bottom of the steps. They stooped, prostrated themselves at the threshold and rubbed its dust on their foreheads. The man Saroj had pointed out was, perhaps, one of the caretakers of the shrine. He was sitting on the ground, surrounded by mounds of rose petals and elaichi dana, and devotees were handing him crumpled ten and twenty-rupee notes. He was accepting their offerings and handing back little packets of blessed elaichi dana and rose petals.

—m—

I watched women light the incense and smear incense ash on their foreheads. I could never consider ash sacred enough to smear on my forehead. Why was I at the shrine, then? The men crowded around the tomb, leaving little space for women to approach. Pigeons fluttered in the dusty shafts of light streaming in from the skylights set in the high green dome. Women were prostrating themselves, weeping silently, swaying as they recited prayers, reading prayer books. Women were jostling to get past the men and close to the tomb to kiss the railing. Some women just sat in silence. I was one of them. One woman was sweeping the floor littered with paper and plastic wrappers from emptied incense packets. Then Saroj took the broom from her.

Soon, I couldn't breathe the thick, incense-choked air and stepped out into the courtyard from where the notes of the qawwal's harmonium could be heard.

—m—

The qawwals were warming up. It was a Thursday in March, a vague kind of day, neither spring nor summer. A tree I saw on my morning walk near the shrine had stopped me with its sudden greenness. I had passed by the same tree a week back and its bare branches and gnarled trunk were nothing to look at. But on that Thursday in March, instead of turning back, like I usually did upon reaching the tree and Malini's tea shack, I stood and stared at the tree. It wore a thick new mantle of green. From the tree, I turned left onto the dirt road. Opposite the temple, where a contaminated tributary of the Ganges flowed into an even more contaminated Ganges, I turned onto the path leading to the shrine. Why? In that moment of turning, I didn't know why. The question didn't arise until much later, when I fumbled for a rational reason.

On the rational plane, I can say I had heard that on some Thursday mornings, a qawwal from the city showed up and sang for a couple of hours at the shrine. I like qawwali, so I went to hear the qawwali. I hadn't gone to petition Chandan Baba. I doubted the supernatural powers of holy men, dead or alive, to intercede on my behalf with God.

I listened to the qawwali for a few minutes and disheartened by the poor quality of singing, placed a twenty-rupee note on the qawwal's harmonium and left. The qawwal kept repeating a few verses in a weak, whiny voice to the accompaniment of anaemic clapping and drum-playing by his assistants. If he was trying to strike fear of life after death in the hearts of his listeners or sow the seeds of repentance in those who forsook Allah's warnings and became immersed in the heedless life of this world, he certainly failed to make any impression on me.

— ∽ —

I decided to leave. I was collecting my sandals from the bottom of the steps when Saroj and Ali joined me. We walked together on the path leading back to the paved road. Saroj walked with a slight limp; the soles of her slippers were worn thin. Beggars, seated on the ground along the path, stretched out their hands, asking for alms in sing-song voices.

I spoke to one with an amputated leg. 'Do you have change for a hundred?'

He nodded vigorously and rummaged under his jute mat, shouted to his neighbours to the right and left and soon, collected coins totalling the sum I needed.

I gave away all the coins, but there were still a few beggars left for whom I didn't have any coins.

We had reached the paved road near the newly greened tree where I had to turn right. Ali hadn't said a word, but Saroj had kept up a steady chatter. 'If I had more money, I would help more people,' she was saying, 'but I only have my bus fare.'

'Your husband?' I asked, trying to assess her situation.

'My husband died and left me nothing, except the shop. My father married me off to him when my mother died. My husband was much older than me. You know how it is. Men and women don't get married. It's money that gets married.'

'I didn't quite think of marriage like that,' I said. 'You're very brave to manage everything on your own.'

I thought of offering Saroj some money, but I didn't.

'Saroj, how did you come to this shrine?' I asked, instead. 'You do know that Chandan Baba was a Muslim saint.'

'Saints are not Hindus or Muslims, don't you know? They're insaan. They help all. Whoever comes to them, they listen to them. What are you?'

'What am I?'

'Hindu? Muslim? Christian?'

I wasn't very sure how to answer her. I had always been aware of the vagueness, the many-layered ambiguities within me. I wanted to say: *there are many of me.*

Instead, I said, 'I don't know. I was born a Muslim, but I'm also just trying to be an insaan.'

'Why did you come here?'

I had a ready-made answer for this one. This one didn't need me to delve deep into ambiguities.

'I came because I wanted to see the shrine and listen to qawwali.'

Saroj shook her head. 'You came because you were called.'

I was intrigued. 'Called by whom?'

'By Baba. I'm not parha-likha like you. Educated people don't believe in these things. You think you came because of the qawwali and I came because my neighbour told me to, but we both came because we were called.'

'I don't feel like I was called. I mean, no, really, I don't believe that.'

'I know you don't. But you wouldn't have come unless you were called. You came to ask for something.'

'I don't think I came to ask for anything. Maybe, if I had more faith… But what could I ask for?'

'For more faith?'

'Do you think he would listen?'

'Why not? If you ask with a pure heart… He always listens to the pure-hearted ones. Maybe, you came because you're lonely?'

'Maybe, but there are so many lonely people out there in the world. I'm not the only one.'

'So why don't you ask him to end your loneliness?'

'Baba? Can he end my loneliness?'

'You have to ask first. Write an arzi.'

—∞—

'I have to go,' I told her. 'This is where I work.'

We had reached the school gate where we had to part.

'You're a teacher?'

'I'm a school counsellor.'

'What is that?'

'I listen to students' problems. I try to help them solve their problems.'

'Arre! Then you're like Baba.'

I was taken aback. 'No! I'm not. I can't work magic like Baba. I listen, I make suggestions, but they have to do the work!'

'We all have to do the work, but no harm in asking for a little help. You write the arzi and hang it next to mine. After my daughter gets married, I'll return with a chadar for his tomb.

I nodded. I realized I hadn't told Saroj my name. Nor had she asked. I had learnt much about her, but what did she know about me?

I turned to give her my name, but changed my mind. If she hadn't asked, maybe, she didn't want to know? Little Ali and Saroj were walking down the road, receding from me. Soon, they had become ghostly figures in the ever-present layer of dust. I felt a twinge of sadness for Saroj, for the way her left leg dragged. I should have offered her the money. I might not ever see this woman again. Would Saroj's leg heal? Would her shop start to do well? Would her older daughter get married and the younger find peace of heart and mind? Saroj and Ali were swallowed by a bend in the road. The dusty road that led to the intersection where Saroj would catch her bus returned to its midday desertedness and I returned to my office.

I walked back with more briskness than usual. I recalled my mental to-do list: a student to see before lunch, a staff meeting right after it; two more students after the staff meeting, followed by yoga, dinner, sleep. I had a routine. I had purpose. I had independence. I had work. I believed my life was under my control, even though there were times I knew it wasn't. Those were lonely times, when I longed for a heart-listener who would reveal to me the real meaning of

my existence. Those were anxious times when I lay awake
and thought my restless questioning would never allow me
respite. I thought of Saroj's words: 'Then you're just like
Baba.' I smiled inwardly. I was not like Baba. I was not a
guru. Listening was all I could offer to those who came to me
in distress. I felt helpless most of the time, despite my outward
guise of unruffled purposefulness. I had no power to change
a single thing in anybody's life, let alone change the world.

A village woman had approached me, because I
happened to be at the shrine at the same time as she was
and I had a notebook and pen in hand. Was that all that had
made our paths cross? There was much that could've made
the meeting not happen: our time of visit could've been
slightly different or our inner and outer resistance could've
prevented us from talking to each other. Her constraints
seemed more material – involving distance and money –
and yet she had overcome more resistance in trusting me
with her life story. My resistance was more mental – the
illogic of petitioning a dead saint or of laying my heart bare
to a village woman.

I didn't write an arzi and take it to the shrine to hang it
next to Saroj's on the string with hundreds of other arzis.
Instead, I hung my arzi in my heart where it still hangs and
continues to grow in length with my growing discontent with
self and world.

I never met Saroj again. I had almost forgotten about
our meeting and only thought of her when I came across
my sketchy notes from that morning's visit to the shrine last
March. I had had only a vague idea of what I wanted to write
about. There seemed nothing significant in our meeting and
yet I had gone on to write about it.

Saroj had her unambiguous, matter-of-fact faith made up
of two mingled faiths. I had my ambiguous, neither-here-
nor-there kind of faith. She was right, though: being on the

path wasn't about being a Hindu or a Muslim. Brokenness wasn't Hindu brokenness or Muslim brokenness.

The path was the path and the destination unattainable, lined with small, chance meetings that led to everyday acts of union, separation and surrender. My path was as torturous for me as Saroj's was for her. Saroj's path had led her to an illusion of certitude, deliverance, faith and hope; mine had led me to a state of heightened bewilderment. I was a sceptic, a dissenting seeker; my path was about detours. And my faith teetered on the borders of faithlessness. You couldn't even call it faith, so filled was it with questions, ambiguity, doubts, hopelessness, arguments, reflection, longings, sadness and a deepening silence.

So what could come of writing about this chance meeting with Saroj? She and I were both in search of the same thing. Or were we? The Beloved who had brought Saroj to the shrine had also taken me there – though I had denied it. Perhaps, it was the Beloved who was prompting me to write about this encounter?

Saroj and I have hung our arzis in a myriad shrines and hearts, in a myriad languages – arzis filled with pain and longing over eons of existence.

A sort of answer to my loneliness is emerging: maybe, some kinds of loneliness aren't meant to end.

12

Ladies Waiting Room

She noticed she was the only passenger in the first-class ladies waiting room. She didn't have a first-class ticket, but looked respectable enough; so who would stop her from entering? There were two blue-uniformed lady guards sprawled out on a large oval dining table. The table was so huge; it looked like a raised double bed. Why were the guards lying on the table? Why was there a bed-like table in a waiting room? She sat down on one of the black metallic chairs nailed to the floor and surveyed the room.

The two guards opened their eyes and glanced at her as if she were an intruder who had encroached on a space reserved for them. Did they think she'd reprimand them for using the waiting room for their afternoon nap? It was a sultry August afternoon and after a long, nauseous bus journey that included several hairpin bends, she had no intentions of asking anybody anything. She was relieved to see no other passengers, no mothers with wailing infants.

She'd been sitting on the black metal chair for quite some time when the breathless, bent-backed coolie barged in. He was the one who had carried her bags and left them at the entrance to the waiting room.

'Are you the one waiting for Tata Muri?' he asked.

'Yes, I am,' she replied. 'Why? What's happened?'

'Tata Muri will be late.'

'How late?'

'I don't know. An hour. Two hours. Who knows? I'll come for your bags when it comes in.'

'Can you bring me a cup of tea? I can't leave my bags here to get it. Here's twenty rupees. You can get one for yourself too.'

'The tea stall is at the other end. I have passengers waiting. It'll take too long.'

'It won't take too long. I would go myself, but I can't leave my bags here.'

She held out the twenty and waited to see if he'd change his mind.

The coolie stood indecisively.

'Okay,' she said. 'Just come back for my bags when the train arrives.'

She was wondering what had made her ask him in the first place. Getting her tea wasn't his job.

'Why won't I come back?' The coolie spoke reproachfully. 'Didn't I come looking for you to tell you your train's late?'

'You did.'

One of the lady guards lying on the table now sat up.

'So you're taking the Tata Muri?' she asked. 'Where to?'

'Allahabad.'

'That's a long way away from here, isn't it? I've never been to Allahabad. I've never even been to Delhi. I haven't been anywhere much. Once, I went with my family to a cousin's wedding in Chandigarh. That's it.'

'But you work for the railways. You can travel easily,' she said.

'That's what people think. We can travel easily, because we work for the railways. But where would we stay if we went to a new place where we didn't know anybody?'

Hotel? The word was on the tip of her tongue.

'You went to Dharamshala?' the other lady guard asked.
She nodded.

'That's where a lot of tourists go.'

She nodded again.

'Where did you stay?' The first guard was continuing the interrogation.

She didn't want to tell them, but didn't want to come across as a snob either. I stayed, she thought of saying, at a hotel, but decided to tell them the truth.

'I stayed at a nunnery.' Then, thinking they wouldn't understand what a nunnery was, she went on to explain, 'It's a place for nuns and women who are interested in meditation and Buddhist teachings.'

'Yes, we know,' said one of the guards. 'We've heard of such places. There are many such places in Dharamshala. How long did you stay there?'

'A month.'

'A month? What did you do there for a month?'

'I stayed in silence.'

'You stayed in silence?'

'Yes. I mean, I read. I wrote. I thought. I listened to the rain and the birds. I looked at the mountains and the green fields. And I watched snails. I thought…well…about all sorts of things I don't think about normally – things I've done and not done and things I could've done differently.'

'You did that for a month?'

She nodded.

'You have children?'

She nodded.

'How did you leave your children for a month?'the first guard asked, looking at her colleague to ascertain if she had expressed the right kind of disapproval. 'We have long duty hours. We come to work at seventy-thirty in the morning. And we work till seventy-thirty at night. We have to go home and cook for our families. Clean. Wash up. Then cook again the next morning. We can't leave our children and go away.'

She kept nodding, but felt the old irritation stir within her. Being asked to explain her choices, getting reprimanded for them, being made to feel self-indulgent, irresponsible. A woman who took off for nunneries. She wanted to explain it wasn't easy. Not as easy as they thought. Then she shrugged off the impulse.

Now the second guard spoke up. 'That's true. We can't even think of taking off like that for a month.'

'No, we certainly can't,' the first guard chimed in. 'Whatever little we earn, we have to spend on our families. We hardly save anything. There are illnesses. There are weddings. It's not easy to do this naukri. We have to work very hard. We do it, because it's our majburi.'

She began to feel nailed to the floor, along with the metal chair. She kept wiping the sweat off her face with a cotton handkerchief that was already soaked. And she continued nodding benignly, warding off her impatience and her impulse to argue with them. She had become a lot calmer after her month at the nunnery. She kept staring up at the creaking ceiling fan as she listened to the guards speak about their hard lives, how they had to cook morning and evening, how they slaved for their children, how they couldn't leave them, how they managed to save so little for contingencies, how difficult it was for them to tide over illnesses and spend on weddings. And how they had no time or money or freedom to go off on her kind of journeys. The fan turned listlessly, almost unwillingly above them...

As soon as the bus had rounded the last curve on the winding mountain road and entered the plains, she had sensed the rise in temperature. It was a warming up of things she was descending into. She sensed the rising wave of disappointment within her. Dust, distrust, crowds and the undercoating of never-ceasing guilt. She stared dispiritedly at the construction workers hacking into the mountainside, making the highways wider and wider to accommodate more tourists and more vehicles. Wider and wider...until?

Unease had come over her even as she was boarding the bus from Dharamshala. A week after she got back home, her daughter would be leaving. The little girl who wanted to give her a hundred kisses on each cheek every night was leaving home. She was no longer little, except in her mother's stubbornly clingy memories. She had come away to the mountains to wash off her memories, instead of fussing over her daughter's home-leaving arrangements. Her unease had morphed into something like menstrual cramps as the bus descended into the plains.

She had left her sparsely furnished little room at the nunnery like she was taking leave of a lover. She had to brace herself to return to her real life, but she wasn't sure what was real. What was supposed to be real seemed highly overrated. When she was finally seated on her assigned berth inside the Tata Muri that departed two hours late, surrounded by people's chatter about their latest obsessions, not wanting to listen to them yapping into their phones and warding off the incessant calls from hawkers of 'Brade, omlette, cutlate!', of 'Chai, chai, masala chai!' and 'Pakora, samosa, Coke, Pepsi, cheeps, cheeps!', she doubted this train was capable of whisking her back to real life.

The moon that had appeared as a faint white spot on the rim of the hills on her last night at the nunnery and grown in radiance as it rose higher and higher, until it hung like a white and grey face in her window, reminded her of a foolish village woman with a wide-eyed smile. From such a moon, what was she to ask? Tell me about real life which I don't know how to inhabit? She thought longingly now of the wise-old-woman-moon and the peepal tree in the nunnery garden. In the evenings, the tree had sparkled with fireflies. During her solitary evenings, she had sat and stared at the fireflies from her window. During her solitary days, she had gazed at terraced fields wearing a fresh coat of green every time it rained. And it had rained almost every day.

On her last night, she had stood in the whitish moonlight streaming in through the curtainless window of her nunnery room. That old-woman-moon had paused in her window, watching her standing by the little desk between her cot and the window. She had sat at this desk and typed her handwritten notes from her spirally bound notebooks into her laptop, notes from books she had browsed through in the nunnery's tiny library. She had said a reluctant farewell to all the things that had constituted her days and nights in her room. And then reproved herself for calling it her room. Her window. Her desk. Her sink, where she had brushed her teeth and looked out of the little side window into the cool, grey, rainy mornings. Her dark green hills. Her half-veiled, mist-topped mountains that had stared back at her in their monkish silence.

—⁂—

The two guards looked at the wall clock and got down from the dining table. They smoothed the creases in their kurtas, took out their pocket mirrors and combs. One rearranged her bindi. The other re-applied kajal.

'We have to get back to work,' one of them said, yawning. 'It's a very hot day.'

'Yes, it must be the hottest day of the year, but we have to get back to work,' the other said. 'We have no choice.'

She kept nodding at them mechanically.

An incoherent announcement crackled over the

loudspeakers:'*Yatrigan, kripya dhyaan den...*' It was difficult to decipher the rest of it.

'Is that the Tata Muri?'she asked the departing women, a little worried, since the coolie had not yet shown up.

'No, no. That's not the Tata Muri,' they reassured her. '*Abhi koi gaadi nahi ayee hai. Aap araam se baitho.* Just relax. We have to get back to work.'

'Wait!'

She rose abruptly and blocked their way, preventing the two women from leaving the waiting room. She had leapt up from her seat with such energy and vehemence that her own action had taken her by surprise.

The two guards looked puzzled. They had assumed she would go on nodding sedately.

'*Kya hua*, madam?'one of them asked, alarmed.

She knew she didn't have much time. She didn't have to prove anything to them, but she felt she had to. They had dismissed her as a first-class AC type who could afford to navel-gaze at a nunnery for a month. She found herself spluttering and tripping over her words.

'You know...you know...I know what you think. I know you think I'm this madam who can just leave her kids. I don't have to do a naukri like you do. I can run away to a nunnery for a month. I can do all this and not worry about a salary. I don't have to save. I don't have to save for weddings and illnesses. But do you know what it's like? I'm not sure you'd like to do what I do, even if you could do it. A month of silence in a nunnery? What do you think? Could you do that?

'But that's not the whole story...It's not just about me having money and running away, okay? A lot of things had to be given up. A lot of people are unhappy. It takes loneliness. And courage. Yes, courage. I haven't talked about how much courage it took. I have a daughter. She's leaving home. She's going away. It's all good; it's all about her future. But she's going away. And I left her and came away. I don't know if you understand what I mean. I'll go into her room. I will hear the school tempo when it pulls up and she won't be the one getting out and ringing the doorbell. Do you know that hollow feeling in your stomach? Do you know what it is to eat lunch sitting next to a blank space? I know I don't have to cook or clean or do dishes every day. I've done it. But I don't have to do it every day.'

The two women looked very confused. 'Madam,' they said, '*aap theek hain? Hum ne aisa kya keh diya*, madam?'

'I'm sorry. I'm sorry...'

She mumbled her way back to the black metallic chair. She had crumbled so easily. It was as if the month at the nunnery had gone to waste.

The two women stared at her. Then they looked at each other and then again at her.

In a somewhat concerned and conciliatory manner, one of them said, '*Aap thak gaye ho na*, madam? *Roti shoti kha ke lambe ho jana yahan.*'They waved towards the recently vacated dining table, urging her to lie down on it and rest. 'Tata Murilate *hi ayegi.*'

She turned away from them. She didn't even see them leave. She stared at the dining table. They were right. Now that they had finally vacated it, it would be good to rest her sweating face and spinning head and aching back on that bed-sized table and lie under the fan.

She climbed onto the table, feeling resigned and contented as she lowered her back onto its hard surface. The thought that she had never felt so lonely crouched up on her. She felt she was about to cry. But she didn't give in to the urge.

The daughter who was leaving, the finger-pointing guards, the mountains and moon and hills and fireflies and the little desk in the room she had mistakenly taken to calling *her* room – now lying there on the dining table in the waiting room under the slowly turning fan, those images came up, one by one, in her drained mind. Slowly, she let them fuse together and become muddled.

13

Kick the Dunya

Her image in the mirror fills her with doubts and thoughts of worthlessness. Will the chiffon kurta with beige and silver embroidery allay doubts? Will it look good enough on her? Will it be appropriate for the walima? It's been some years since she bought or wore formal clothes. There is no need, as she has stopped going to weddings and parties. But this reception is different. She has decided to go, because it is the walima of a young man who is the son of her father's friend. And it will be an opportunity to take her mother out, her mother who never goes out at all, unless it is to see the doctor.

Normally, she showers and dresses before stepping out of the bathroom, but today, she steps out and stands before the mirror in her bedroom, wrapped in a towel. In the pale light filtering in through the drawn curtains, she unveils herself to herself. As the towel drops to the floor, her aged body's softened, flaccid contours come into view. She recalls the earlier tautness of those curves, the suppleness and shapeliness of a bygone era. And though this body is not obese or stooped or unattractive, she feels a vague loss of confidence overcome her.

She likes to do things in an orderly way. So she starts from the top. Greying and brittle though it is, she still has a head of abundant hair. She had once thought of dyeing it, but decided against it. Why should she hide her greyness? Some of her friends had started losing their hair right after menopause, but though her hair lacks softness and lustre, she has enough of it. Her eyes. She's always been rather short-sighted, but for a decade now, she's also had to use reading glasses. Her almond-shaped eyes had once held a sparkle, but they've grown rounder and smaller with age and lie half-buried between the folded skin of her eyelids and the puffy bags beneath. The mouth. Two lines descend from the nostrils to her mouth, making her face a divided territory. The lips. Still plump, still passable, perhaps, kissable. The chin is a double chin. The neck. Wrinkles criss-cross it and are especially prominent when she tilts her head up or swallows. She swallows now and notices the sudden appearance of wrinkles in the middle of her neck. Breasts. The sag is undeniable. Her nipples have strayed downwards below the midline of the bra. Arms. There are three bulges on her right arm. Harmless lipoma, the doctor said, when she consulted him, bothered by their first appearance. Now she finds newer lumps every so often on her upper arms. They tell her that smoothness is not forever. Belly. A definite bulge there has replaced earlier flatness and firmness.

In the dark triangle of pubic hair are telltale white hairs. Her vagina used to be a source of anxiety, mixed with yearning, that had tormented her for long. Its incomprehensible, unintelligible yearnings had made her restless and sexual encounters with the one man in her life had not stilled those yearnings. But menopause and disenchantment with love and life have made those unsettling yearnings settle down. *There's a downward pull to everything about me*, she thinks. Body and mind, everything seems to be succumbing. Her thighs lack firmness and protrude like plump chicken legs below her hips. Knobby knees and bow-legged calves. And at the end of her feet are ten misshapen toes. She had never liked her feet.

They reminded her of her mother's feet. She holds up her hands and stares at their reflection in the mirror. The veins on the back of her hands stand out – thick, bulging tributaries of a river. The skin of her hands is fractured into a myriad furrows in a craggy landscape.

I am a pear-shaped body, she thinks disparagingly, *disproportionately bottom-heavy. I'm a dying civilization. I'm a museum housing relics of an ancient civilization. I'm visiting this museum for the first time, even though I've been living in it for half a century.*

She moves away from the mirror, turns on the table lamp and sits down on the edge of her bed, staring at the skin of her wrinkled hands in the yellow light. There's something sad and spellbinding about these hands, she thinks, fondly feeling their leathery, weathered beauty. Now that the skin isn't stretched tight over bones and muscle, it has acquired that which only time brings about. It's like a filled notebook and on it is scrawled the faded script of her life. She discerns something akin to love for the old skin of her hands. Age has moulded it into leatheriness. The right hand is more lined and leathery and has more prominent veins on it than the left, the left being her less-used hand. She is gently awakened by the slow change that has come over her, change that she hadn't given such meticulously loving attention to before.

She clasps her bra, propping up the nipples into place just above the midline of the bra. Then she slips on the cream-coloured slip, followed by the beige chiffon kurta and the small zircon earrings she has unearthed from a drawer in her closet. Tea-coloured lipstick and a dab of perfume on her wrists – a gift from her daughter on her last birthday. She's not sure how she appears to others. It's impossible to say if one appears the same to others as one appears to oneself. And even if one trusts the way one appears to oneself in the mirror, how reliable is that image? Something about scrutinizing her body in the mirror has made her realize the impossibility of knowing what one truly looks like.

—∽—

She goes to find her mother who has managed to get herself into a silk outfit without much help from her. They leave the house – two elegantly dressed, respectable old ladies. Returning home to live with her parents after her rebellious 'love' marriage ended, she had been grateful for their ailments; they had prevented excessive probing into what went wrong between her husband and her. What had seemed like misfortune, at first, had turned out to be a silent, mutually beneficial agreement between her parents and her. And after her father's death, her mother's increasing dependence on her had only helped matters.

They give the driver the address and she settles back and watches the city's late-evening frenzy from the car window. It's a long drive from the genteel south to the undignified northern part of the city, which is more like several cities hastily cobbled together. It's a long drive from the tight-lipped, gated guardedness of bungalows of the south side to the unguarded, crowded, unsafe apartment buildings of the north. The billboards and tall buildings dedicated to cushioning the docility of the privileged glide past as the car negotiates the serpentine flyovers linking the south to the north.

After an arduous, hour-long drive – entering and exiting the many flyovers, the smoke-filled, traffic-packed streets, navigating through the darkness and puddles of rain-muddied roads, the overflowing sludge from the unexpected showers of the past few days, the stagnant water, manoeuvring past impatient cars, unruly buses, menacing trucks and tired men on motorbikes – their arrival at the wedding venue seems bereft of a sense of reaching a destination. She feels exhausted after the ride through a city that is an overstretched empire. It's no longer a city that connects people to places.

The driver stops outside the gigantic lit-up tent. A row of such tents, converted into wedding halls, line the street. They are entering one of many weddings taking place on that street on that particular night. A different, yet similar wedding is taking place inside each tent. Inside the wedding tent they enter, there's the similitude of splendour and a ghastly sort of glamour, underscored by chandeliers and plastic flowers in large plastic urns, reminiscent of the weddings shown in the TV serials her mother loves to watch.

She had left home with the naiveté of doing a lower middle-class family a favour by attending their son's walima, but the sight of the chandeliers, the red-carpeted aisle, the crisp tablecloth-covered tables jolts her. She's filled with even more doubt than before. First of all, she must make sure they have come to the right wedding. She takes out the wedding card from her purse and asks a woman at the entrance. The woman smiles and nods and points out the groom's mother, who rushes to meet them. They are led to a table and the groom's mother sits with them to keep them company. She looks ill at ease in her stiff silk sari and the pallu keeps sliding off her head. A vase filled with plastic flowers topples over. The table wobbles as they sit down. The groom's mother looks embarrassed. She smiles as if to say: *this is the best we could do*. She has the demeanour of a confused little girl. Shyness and lack of self-assurance are evident from the shaky way in which she sets the vase right and keeps rearranging her sari pallu.

She enquires of the groom's mother where her father's friend, the groom's father, is. She shrugs and looks away.

'*Nahi aye. Pata nahi kyun nahi aye*,' she mumbles and looks down into her lap.

How can this elderly woman, the mother of so many

children, be so diffident, so unsure? The certitude and knowledge that come from being loved and valued are absent. Her mother starts asking about the bride, her bridal outfit. The groom's mother replies in low tones. She says she chose the bride for her son and she also chose the bride's pink and silver walima outfit.

Plastic chandeliers and plastic roses are ill-placed in the tent that is yet to fill with people, though it is almost ten o'clock. The bride and groom are busy posing for the photographer and videographer, smiling self-consciously into the cameras. They look like the stars of a show that is destined to be soon over.

The guests finally start trickling in. The photographers and videographers can now take pictures of people other than the bride and groom. They assume importance, waving obstructing persons aside, asking guests to pose, giving them instructions – lean in, smile, stand closer together – making it seem worthwhile for the groom's family that has poured all its savings and borrowings into this reception.

Guests move, cameras click and women smile, expecting to be noticed and photographed. Time and money are immortalized through refashioning the humdrumness of existence. Everybody is conspiring in stamping out everydayness. Intentional forgetfulness has forged a bond among the guests and the hosts. A revolt is on against the familiar. The humming vertical air conditioners along the walls and the chandeliers pouring down yellow light, the plastic flowers, the high-backed love-seat, the creamy silk on the sofas have all been made complicit in the revolt.

Fingering her small zircon earrings, which she thought were quite elegant when she put them on, she now muses over her own drabness in this simulated splendour. A middle-aged woman with her elderly mother, seated at a wedding where hardly anyone cares to know them. The groom's mother has risen and moved away from their table to welcome the other guests and is showing them to vacant tables on either side of the crimson-carpeted aisle. The noise of human chatter is growing louder and louder. She catches glances of quick appraisal and dismissal of herself and her mother from the newly arriving guests. Nobody sits too long at their tables. There's constant movement, incessant talking and clicking of phone cameras. Long jhumkas dangle from earlobes and restless women run their hands through their hair and pout into their phones.

Suddenly, the chandeliers dim and coloured ceiling lights come on. There's a momentary hush inside the tent. Then circles of green and red light dart across the now-greenish tent walls. She rests her head against the back of her chair and imagines she is sinking to the bottom of a green ocean. An orange cloth behind the love-seat flutters like a flame as the blast of breeze from a fan fixed to the floor hits it. The DJ turns up the volume on the latest Bollywood hit and she tries to remember the words as Atif Aslam's quivering voice rises above the chatter of guests.

O tere sang yara...tu raat divani...mai zard sitara
Mai tera ho jaon jo tu kar de ishara...
Tujhpe mar ke hi to mujhe jeena aya hai
Mai behta musafir to tehra kinara...

O, my beloved, you are the ecstatic night,
I am the yellow star.
I become yours the instant you command me to.
I have learnt to live by dying for you.
I am the drifter, you are the steady shore.

At the show's finale, just before the lights come on, the bride and groom reappear at the entrance. The skittish photographer walks and skips a few steps ahead of them.

The bride smiles in the green light and treads in her high heels, supported by the black-sleeved arm of the groom. They are performers who, it seems, will go their separate ways at the end of the show. The videographer keeps walking backwards, approaching the stage, carrying the heavy camera on his slim shoulders. She starts feeling sorry for him, his frailness and his long hours of work. She wonders when he'll get home to his family. The beads and pearls and sequins on the bride's pink and silver outfit sparkle like a phooljhari. As the couple reach the stage, a mist envelops them from a mist-releasing device at the foot of the stage. Covered in mist, they are also showered with foam from a foam-releaser. Is the foam meant to be snow, she wonders. The bride and groom climb onto the stage, turn their faces to their audience and smile.

Now the green lights are turned off and the chandeliers shine their harsh light on everything once again. The bride and groom are now seated on the stage, receiving guests who are lining up to congratulate them, give them their envelopes of money and have their photos taken with the pair. The guests who are not on the stage are clicking selfies.

She guides her mother up to the stage to hand over their envelope. The groom takes the envelope and hastily stuffs it into his pocket, uttering a brisk 'thank you'. There's a quick click of the camera and it's time for them to move aside for the next-in-line guest. She holds her mother's arm to steady her and they return to their table to wait for dinner to be served.

All that fretting and planning over clothes, the lingering before the mirror, the time wasted over getting dressed, the long drive – for this? She glances at her mother's somewhat confused face and feels lost herself, as if something vital had been squandered in coming here. The white-uniformed bearers are pouring hot water into the food warmers. It won't be too long before dinner is served. And as soon as dinner is over, she wants to leave.

Finally, the men uncover the tureens and platters of food and stand guard behind the buffet tables. The guests pile up their plates with rice and naan and fried chicken and curried chicken and *achari* chicken and fried fish. Every plate is piled with more food than one person can eat. She makes a plate for herself and one for her mother. They eat very little, take hasty leave of the groom's mother and get into the car for the long drive home. Her mother says the food was terrible and she doesn't know how they could afford such an expensive affair. And the worst thing is, the food wasn't palatable after all that money spent. She nods, immensely grateful for not being inside that tent any more.

The next day, she calls up her father's friend. He used to visit their house every Sunday to read the newspaper and have breakfast with her father, arriving by an early morning bus and leaving after lunch. But a few years back, he was pushed off the bus by an impatient crowd and broke his leg. His Sunday visits had stopped after that accident.

'Salaam, Uncle! Why weren't you there at the walima yesterday?'

His words are slurred, bordering on incoherence. She has to turn on the phone's speaker.

'Don't call me Uncle,' she hears him say.

She's amused. 'What should I call you, then?'

'Call me Arif.'

'It won't be respectful. You're so much older.'

'Does age mean the heart and mind have also aged?'

'No, but…it would be disrespectful.'

'I'm telling you to call me by my name.'

'Okay, I'll call you Arif Sahib. Tell me, why didn't you

come to the walima, Arif Sahib? I was hoping to meet you there.'

'I don't go to weddings and walimas.'

'But it was your son's walima!'

'I especially wasn't going to attend my son's walima. I didn't even go to my granddaughter's wedding. They're all against me. If I showed up, they'd insult me. They say I'm old-fashioned. I used to scold my sons and sometimes, I beat them. Why? For not studying. For lying. For stealing. For staying out late with useless boys. Did I do wrong? I didn't drink or waste time with other women. Did I go gambling? So where did I go wrong? Why do they treat me like this?'

'It must be tough for you.'

'They think I'm mad. They are against me, because I don't live the way they want me to. So I've left them. I kicked them out, before they could kick me out.'

'But doesn't it get lonely? Living alone?'

'Loneliness is better. It's peaceful. I don't have to put up with anybody's insults. Tell me, how's your Ammi?'

'She hardly ever goes out, so I forced her to accompany me to the walima. She's worried.'

'About what?'

'About everything. The past. The future.'

'She hasn't kicked the world. She still remembers who-did-what and who-said-what to her half a century ago. Tell her to kick the dunya. Kick her past. That's the only way to get rid of her worries.'

'Yes...she does live a lot in her past.'

'Tell her to kick the world like I did.'

'I don't know if she wants to.'

Suddenly, he changes the subject. 'Do you know, yesterday, I was cleaning the stove. Remember the stove?'

'The stove! Yes, the stove. You still have it? Does it still work?'

'Of course it works! I will keep cleaning it and making it work as long as I live. Every time I clean it, you're with me; you're standing right next to me.'

'I remember I got it for you. But that was years ago. I was hoping to meet you at the walima. I would come and see you, but I can't drive in this city and the driver isn't always available.'

'No...don't come to see me, Chaand. This city's very unsafe. Oh, sorry! I called you Chaand. Did you notice?'

'It's okay,' she says, uncertain about how she should react.

'Can I call you Chaand? You don't mind? I don't know why I called you Chaand... It slipped from my tongue. I know you're from another world. You're not like these other people. I know you. I know what you think.'

'Really? What do you think I think?'

'I won't tell you, but I know what you think!' She hears him chuckle.

'How do I know you really know what I'm thinking?' she asks.

He switches topics. 'Do you know how old I am?'

'Eighty-three?'

'No! Ninety-three. I'm ninety-three years old. And I won't live much longer.'

'Ninety-three? Mashallah!'

'And you just added more years to my life by calling me. Why did you do that? I don't want to live too long.'

'Why not? Not everybody makes it to ninety-three. You should be proud of it.'

'I am up at two a.m. Can't sleep. I stare at the ceiling and the ceiling fan and the four walls. I stare at them for hours till it's light. At six a.m., I turn on the radio to listen to the Quran recitation. I make tea. I eat. I read the paper. I work on my fretsaw. I eat. I go to bed by eight p.m. What should I go on living for, you tell me?'

'You have your own place. You're not a burden on anybody. You can take care of yourself. That's why. Who cooks for you?'

'I cook for myself. Chicken necks. Much cheaper than chicken. It takes a long time to clean and cook. Hundred rupees a kilo. But I only buy half a kilo at a time. Lasts me for four meals.'

'I don't know anybody who can cook for himself at ninety-three!'

Plucking feathers off chicken necks...she imagines him standing at his sink and feels a sudden onrush of nausea and pity. Imagines him haggling over the price of half a kilo of chicken necks at a squalid roadside stall, then trudging home with a plastic bag of chicken necks dangling by his side, the arduous climb up the five flights of stairs, hobbling on his not-fully-healed leg, bending over a basin filled with chicken necks in greasy, bloodstained water. Suddenly, she feels there's nothing common between them and their conversation is futile. She's irritated that he has taken the liberty to call her Chaand, but she can't end the call abruptly.

'Does your wife live with you?' she asks.

'We can't live together under one roof. She's an illiterate woman. Can't tell a five hundred-rupee note from a thousand-rupee note. She prefers to live with her sons.'

But you didn't mind having all those kids with this illiterate woman. She manages not to blurt out the words. Instead, she says gently, 'Don't you take the bus into the city any more?'

'Rarely. But I'll come over if you want to meet me one of these days.'

'Do call me when you plan to come over.'

'Why should I have to call you?'

'I don't want you to come all the way and not find me at home.'

'I'll find you, no matter where you are. I'm the modern Robinson Crusoe.'

She laughs.

He continues, 'You respect me. I respect you. This is the best thing. That's how it should always be.'

Then he starts rambling, losing track of time and logic. She says she has to go, because it's time to have lunch with her mother.

—∽—

After her morning walk, she settles down on her meditation cushion. And suddenly, the word, 'Chaand,' interferes with her daily recitations. He had called her Chaand. By mistake? He had apologized for the transgression, as if he realized he had overstepped his boundaries. It was an impulsive, unguarded slip by a ninety-three-year-old man whose mind was slippery. It wasn't about her looks. He couldn't know what she looked like now. It had been years since he had seen her. He said he knew she wasn't like others. Then why Chaand?

During her morning meditation, Chaand ushers her into unvisited places, lifting veils off her, revealing her inner gardens to her. Inside her flesh-and-bone body, she picksher steps luxuriously over her courtyard gardens. She is the full moon, brimming with benevolence. She is a bowed-down tree, abundant with her own fruit. She is the sensuous lotus in the pond, a nymph bathed by her own cool, silvery moonlight. Trees and flowers and birds and flowing flasks of wine surround her. Bathed by her own healing light, she is a tall, stately cypress tree, wrapped in silk and velvet. She is the queen of her inner queendom, reclining upon a divan. A queen in her own universe, her bahisht, her heaven.

She has flaws, shortcomings of body and mind. She has been bothered by her flaws, her bulges, her broadening and flattening body; where there had been curves, now there are bulges. Flaws she used to wish she could fix until a few years ago. Thighs, nose, breasts... Nothing about her is perfect. Nor was it so in the past. She had spent her youth sizing herself up and falling short. Nagging doubts about her imperfections, not being able to attract the attention of the right sort of man had preoccupied her for many years, before she finally agreed to marry the man who seemed the best of the lot from the few proposals she received.

But there were also flaws of the mind which she felt she couldn't right, no matter how hard she tried. She was intelligent and hard-working in high school and she had believed she would go on to achieve success in some profession. But she hadn't. She had nothing to show for all the exams she excelled in. Neither had she performed well in the marriage. Everything about her seemed fair-to-middling, diffuse, uncertain and somehow, extinguished.

She often delves into her past now, comparing herself to her less-talented classmates. She hasn't kept in touch with them. She doesn't know how she would compare with them now. So she has kept away from Facebook. Mental portraits of herself as a successful woman, portraits of herself she had constructed in her younger years, still haunt her, taunt her.

You have to kick the world – she recalls Arif Uncle's words. He had said that about her mother. But she could use the advice. Kick the world. Kick the past. When will she stop seeing herself in the mirror of the world?

That word, 'Chaand,'has flung open locked doors to some hidden knowledge. She is still trapped in the world of weddings and walimas, but there is this sudden knowledge she couldn't have conveyed to herself or to anyone in words which has come to her with a certainty. It's nothing more than a feeling. A sentiment. A mood. So what will now be different about her and the world she has been living in? A nondescript, grey-haired, middle-aged woman like her, unwillingly wading her way through? But no, the knowledge is, in a way, negating this: she isn't the nondescript, grey-haired woman she believed she was, even though she appears to be just that to herself and the world. The sudden knowledge that has come to her has unveiled rivers and gardens to her. It has emboldened her, pushed her ahead with love and longing towards what she can't express. But it is something elemental, something so fundamental that only by stumbling into it – after feeling lost among cars and crowds and dust and dejection – can she let go of the labels that have defined her and arrive at this essence of herself.